Mall Dweller

By

C.D. GRUBER

ISBN: 978-0692393895
ISBN-10: 0692393897
LCCN: 2015910978

This book is dedicated to my beautiful children
Jack and Hannah

Special thanks to Aimee Avery for all of her help.

Contents:

1
BONFIRE

BODIE HOUGE STARED AT THE DYING EMBERS of the homecoming bonfire. To the casual observer it may have looked as though Bodie was simply day dreaming, but in reality his life was passing before his very eyes. Last year at this time he had beat out a senior for the starting position of quarterback. He had earned it, amazing everyone when he got that desperately needed first down that Altamont High just couldn't come down with just weeks before. It all came so easy. But this year it was different. The job was his, no doubt about that, but a 'what-have-you-done-for-me-lately' syndrome had emerged. His numbers were not as high as last year's, the big seniors that had blocked for him last year were gone and even though the wins kept coming, the stories 'above the fold' on the first page of the sports section were now below it. During the World Series, Altamont High's exploits weren't even on the first page.

"Ready for a long day?"asked C.J.. Bodie woke up, turning slowly to CJ, his longtime center and friend. He was a pudgy blonde kid that never quite grew up but was always there for him, during the good and the bad.

"Fremont isn't going to just lay down for us. And then there's the Homecoming Dance. Are you and Chrissy going to be King and Queen again this year?"

"Don't even remind me of the dance." said Bodie tersely. "If I could abdicate my monarchy I would in a heartbeat. Chrissy doesn't want it, I don't want it... to hell with it. It's meaningless."

"Well, this year the football players don't vote on it alone... everyone does. So you just might get your wish!" CJ responded enthusiastically.

"Good. I don't need the headache," exhaled Bodie. "I wish I could be done with it all."

"What's wrong?"

"I dunno," sighed Bodie. "This year. It's different... I dunno. A lot of expectations. Bettencourt already has a verbal with Stanford. Can you believe that? Shit. I haven't had anyone give me a verbal offer. Lately no one has even given me a sales pitch. I'm starting to get scared, man."

"Bodie baby: it's October. Not February. There's plenty of time. Don't freak out. Hang in there baby!"

"Yeah. Okay." There was a sign of resignation in his voice. Bodie was a good looking kid, about six foot one, and, perhaps, still growing. He had good chiseled features, longer brown hair with streaks of sun-bleached strands. "I'll wait for the offers to roll in."

In the world of high school football, the senior year was where the rubber met the road. A lot of players would not get a full ride scholarship to a Football Bowl Series school. Or even a Football Championship Series level school. Some may have nothing left but a junior college tryout and then... pray for death.

"If it makes you feel any better, I haven't gotten any scholarship offers yet, either." assured CJ.

"Hang in there, baby," said Bodie. "There's hope for us yet." They shared a laugh and decided to go to the food court in the mall.

"I'll meet you there at ten." yelled Bodie as he walked toward one small group in the dwindling crowd. Bodie had been coming to the homecoming bonfire for four years now, and he had always noticed the oldsters that would show up, alumni from years gone by. One group always stuck out in his eye; they were gray now, some balding, but some still letting their freak flag fly, albeit cropped a little shorter.

"I feel like I should know you guys... you're here every year. I'm Bodie. Bodie Houge."

"Ahh. Mr. QB..." The small group grinned and gave each other sidelong glances. They wore Columbia outdoor gear or sport coats. One had wire rim glasses as if it were still the sixties, but they weren't that old. The others had Italian frames, the pricey ones. But they all still wore jeans. Bodie liked that. They all shook hands.

"Too bad Randy isn't here. He was QB when we went here. He used to come, but he moved to Idaho someplace. Sandpoint?" He looked at the others- they didn't know. "Had enough of California, I guess. Tax burden and all."

"You guys CPA's?" Bodie asked, half serious.

"Naw. Jeremy's an English professor at Sonoma State;

Terry does sound at Channel Eight. The rest of us have run-of-the-mill jobs... nothing that involves an executive jet or anything." There were chuckles all around.

"I guess I have my life all ahead of me... and all that." Bodie offered with a little hesitation.

"You really do, with all joking aside. You do." said the wire-framed alum. "You gonna play college ball? I think you can. You run around like Joe Montana did. You always seem to find someone."

"Well, I'll wait and let the offers pour right in... I'll see." Bodie didn't like the subject. It was beginning to be a bit of concern, to say the least. And his grades. The grades! They wouldn't earn him a ticket into college, not on their merits alone. They may not even allow him to play out the second quarter here in high school.

"I bet you guys got a lot of high school memories. They must be all coming back now." chided Bodie, attempting to change the subject.

"No, not really." they said in unison and laughed, grinning at each other. "Just getting high and seeing who could drink the most beer. Only Jeremy played football. The rest of us just watched from the stands. Watching Randy. The team did okay. Seven and three? I can't remember." The wire-framed glasses guy drew a drag on his cigarette.

Terry spoke up. "Well, there was one game we didn't spend the end of in the stands."

Two of the others had been sneaking snorts out of pint bottles and began smiling knowingly.

"Charter Stockton." They all nodded.

"Mmmmm!." Jeremy slowly pointed his index finger while holding his pint and swallowing. His semi-frizzie hair had streaks of gray and bounced as he nodded. "They had it coming!"

"What about Charter Stockton?" Bodie asked. Charter Stockton was still in Altamont High's league, but not for long. It was just getting too big to play in division II football. They were rumored to be moving up to division I.

Jeremy offered Bodie a swig of his pint and he took a guzzle. It didn't go down very smoothly. He peeked at the label. 'Old Yellowstone.'

"You remember the 'Stones at Altamont?" asked Jeremy. Bodie vaguely remembered there had been a huge Woodstock-like concert at the speedway, up in the hills above Altamont and Tracy. Way back in the 70's he thought.

"The Stones had hired the Hell's Angels to do security at this big-assed concert. Maybe it was the promoters, who didn't know how to run a giant concert. Anyway; some dumb-ass pulls a gun on the Hell's Angels and, surprise, gets himself killed. It upset the band and, to this day, they never play 'Gimmie Shelter', the song that they were playing at the time, live, ever again. So, some years go by and then our high school marching band is practicing "Gimmie Shelter" and people at school said maybe we shouldn't be playing that song, live, either. So it was a big thing, in the school paper and maybe the Chronicle, so it was decided the band wouldn't play 'Gimmie Shelter.'"

"Yeah... I think I remember that." Bodie said, in a hush.

"So, long story short, we play Charter Stockton, lose, and as we're saying our song with the crowd on our side of the stadium, here's their band striking up "Gimmie Shelter" with little smirks on their tuba-playing lips. We were pissed off as it was, losing by twenty and all, and we just all started running to their side of the field. Not just the players. The band, the student body-- everybody. It was weird."hkl

"Yeah. It was weird," chimed in the wired-framed guy. "For some reason no one had left the stands. Twenty point loss, and just about everyone was still there for the song, like they knew they should stick around. And now, like, everyone is jogging over to their band. Even me! I'm no head knocker, man. But everyone knew we had to go over there."

"Before you knew it, trombones and trumpets were making wa-wa sounds and drowning out as they got their butts kicked all around the sideline. Their football team had no clue as to what was going on, but they came back, some from out of the tunnel, and started punching back. Their coaches took a long time to come back and figure out what was going on," Jeremy said, trying not to laugh.

"Bedlam, man! Pure and simple!" shouted wire-frame guy.

"Wow..." Said Bodie, shaking head almost laughing. "What happened? National Guard?"

"Eh, lots of broken noses, busted teeth. Then the two cops watching the melee pulled out their night sticks and started whacking heads. They did that in those days. Our coaches got in the middle and pushed us around. Their coaches dragged key players into the tunnel. But the band kept play'n, if you know what I mean."

Terry was showing the others a scar he got from a nightstick.

A sweet feminine voice called out to Bodie. "Hey Houge: let's get pizza, damn it." A blonde-haired girl trudged through the sandy soil up to where Bodie was. She wore a white ski parka that hugged her slinky figure. The Delta Breeze ruffled the fake fur fringe on the hood. "Can I have my boyfriend back? We're getting hungry over there." She nodded to a few stragglers past the dying bonfire.

"This is Christine, guys."

"Go ahead, Bodie," said the wire-framed guy. "Sober up with the pizza."

"Nice talking with you guys-- that was funny!"

With that the alums all turned and straddled the sandy turf. They were headed toward a couple of Range Rovers.

"Tying one on with the oldsters, huh?" teased Christine.

"Yeah. I guess I did." Bodie smiled as he butted foreheads with Christine. "Hey, where did Chase go, anyway? He was here at the beginning and then he just plain disappeared."

"He left early for the Mall. Long time ago. Come on; let's catch up with him, Bodie-man!"

2
THE HIGHS AND LOWS OF
HIGH SCHOOL PARTICIPATION

THE PRE-GAME LOCKER ROOM WAS A ROWDY PLACE.
Everyone batted the metal 'Highlander Football' sign that had
hung there for thirty years. Coach Ramsey had posted the
opponent's name on his dry erase board for everyone to see
since last Monday. It was no surprise; everyone had memorized
the fall schedule last May. It was just a way to get focused.
Tonight they played Fremont Union. Not a team to fear.
Fremont Union was struggling to maintain a .500 average.
Their running game was their strength, but every other facet of
their game was mediocre. Coach Ramsey tried to keep their
guard up, but it wasn't working. Confidence was high.

The hoots and hollars suddenly died down. Most
everyone could see Coach Ramsey in his office giving gear and
pads to the new player. She gave her back to the plate glass
window, realizing some of the team was in various stages of
disrobing. She had a blonde ponytail braided halfway down.
She was not tall, a little stocky, but still had an athletic build. It
was no secret she wanted on the team, and as a Quarterback no

less. But Ramsey didn't want her. But in the 21st Century, there was no stopping a determined girl who did not have a girl's football team to participate on. In fact, in California, it was the law. She had to be admitted to the team.

"Hester's made the team, man," said CJ. "Not that Ramsey had any say in the matter. He thought he could string her along by letting her practice, but the boosters threatened to get the ACLU involved. After three weeks of drills and practice, I guess I woulda demanded a jersey, too."

"Thanks. Now she's going to take my job away," Bodie offered.

"Yeah... right. Coach had her taking field goal snaps all week. She's just a back-up for Harrison."

Harrison Bruce was Bodie's back-up. He was a smart guy, could remember pass patterns and looked good in practice, but wasn't good under pressure. He would throw interceptions, get sacked, and was slow at reading defenses. He wasn't ever going to beat out Bodie for the starting position, so he held the ball for place kicking. His hands were okay, but there were some close calls.

"Did you see what coach had her doing yesterday?" asked Chase Bettencourt while he laced up his uniform. "Coach had her kicking field goals. She was makin' 'em, too!"

"Really," said Bodie, in disbelief. "How far?"

"Eh. I dunno. Twenty, twenty five yards out, I guess."

"From the goal line?"

"No. From the post." With that Chase grabbed his helmet and joined the others who finished dressing. They were waiting for Coach Ramsey's pep talk.

CJ looked at Bodie. "Maybe she's got a spot on this team after all."

"Brett Heckler might have a problem with that," protested Bodie. Brett was the kicker and also took care of the punter duties. He was an average all around kicker.

Someone came from behind Bodie and lifted him up by his braced elbows.

"Coach wants all lame-asses to the talk. You hurry. You get ass to talk." It was Jocko, the only big hause on the offensive line, next to CJ. Every other really big guy graduated last year. Jocko would keep the heat off of Bodie on critical third downs.

"If I could get my ass to talk I'd be all over the internet," Bodie laughed.

"Bodie smart ass. Get to talk. Now." Jocko laid the caveman accent on heavily as he and C.J. raised Bodie at the elbows, locked. Instinctively, Bodie froze in his kneeling position as they carried him away to the the meeting area. It was always crowded when everyone gathered in.

"Coach keeps trying to even out the running game with the passing game," lamented Bodie. "It's cutting into my numbers. Getting me off a rhythm. He's trying to pound a square peg in a round hole. Marcus is a great open field runner, but he's not big enough to run North/South. He can't run over anybody. We don't have enough big guys to pop open holes for him. Not like last year. Coach is afraid of a lot of things. He wants the stats to show a balanced offense. But it won't happen. This is his first year and he's responding to pressure."

"Marcus' dad?"

"Yeah. And maybe because he doesn't want to be accused of not playing him enough because he's black."

"These days? Come on!"

"Well, it's all politics sometimes. "He'd do better to have Marcus run patterns out of the backfield. Ahh. Coach doesn't listen to me. He's afraid of taking advice from a seventeen year old."

"Let's hear what he has to say."

"Listen up gentlemen!" Coach Ramsey was trying to get them to settle down. "I'd like to welcome a new teammate. Everyone give a warm welcome to Hester Sargeant." He clapped his hands high over his head, encouraging everyone else to do the same. A shy girl came in toward the middle of the group, at Coach Ramsey's insistence. The team was loud and shouted their approval. Bodie clapped politely. "Hester is going see some action later in the season, to help out on punting duty. Brett will continue on with field goals and kickoffs. Let's give her all the support we can. Hester: welcome."

She got pats on the shoulder pads and all that. She smiled reluctantly. She had a few freckles on her nose and cheeks. Almost no makeup. But she was still cute. It was abundantly clear to all that there would be no slaps on the ass if she angled a great punt. There was an awkwardness in the air all around her.

"Okay lady and gentlemen: Fremont Union. They're hungry. Watch out for hungry teams."

Coach Ramsey was in his late thirties, thin like a cross country runner. His nose was slender and eyes deep set in his sockets. His chin protruded from his face, but it wasn't a manly jaw, just a skinny chin. Bodie thought that although he projected his voice and was over six foot two, Coach Ramsey was a scared little man.

"This is a league game and we both know if you want into CIF postseason play, you have to be the best in your own league... or very near to the top. They know they have to beat us to have a chance at the post season. A win would put them over .500. They're hungry and I know it. We need this win, too. The two non-league losses can haunt us if we're waiting for a CIF invitation. We're going to shut down this running game of theirs and open ours up."

After a short pause, coach Ramsey shouted: "What's going on here!"

"Highlander Football!" The thundering response was loud, proud and brief.

"Johnny." The assistant, Coach Patterson, showed some video of Fremont Union's offensive plays. Plays they've watched almost all week. It was clear to Bodie that Coach was going to run more and pass less. His numbers were going to suffer.

Vs. Fremont Union High

The clash of pads and grunts deafened Bodie's ears. The linemen were grinding it out. Bodie had handed off to Marcus and he had hesitated just before the line; there was no hole. No place to go. Bodie was thunderstruck when, for a split second, Marcus actually turned his head back to look at Bodie. Everyone at the line, hell, the entire stadium, knew what Altamont was going to do. Or at least try. Bodie was depressed that the playbook was about half as thick as it was last year. A lot of it was now running plays. Running plays that fooled no one.

Marcus was small by even high school standards, and without a line making holes for him he was not moving the sticks. Fremont Union was zeroing in on Altamont's running game and shutting it down completely. Marcus was slammed down on his back, right in front of Bodie. Marcus was slow getting up, this time like a turtle trying to get his off his back. Bodie just stood there, tired of helping him get up. Instead his gaze fixed on Ted Studemire, the tight end. Ted was just running through the motions, sometimes just jogging out his routes. Most of Bodie's passes were to his wideouts. If he ever threw to Ted, it was in desperation, using him as a safety valve. But tonight was even worse. Bodie was only passing to take the heat off of Marcus; no one was in sync, even after three quarters. They just weren't passing enough. It was fourth down, but this time Hester came in to punt instead of Brett.

Hester angled her punt away from the return men. It was a little shallow; there w e r e moans of disappointment in the crowd. But it took a wicked bounce behind the linemen and kept bouncing toward the sideline. By the time a return man got his hand on it, it had rolled deep enough for a 38 yard punt, at least on paper. There were finally cheers coming from the crowd.

Bodie was pissed. It was almost the fourth quarter and they were trailing, seven to three. Coach Ramsey seemed like he wasn't going to change a thing.

"Coach this ain't happening." Bodie barked at him. He wasn't asking now, he was ordering.

"We have to put the ball in the air, or we're going to lose a close, ugly game." Coach Ramsey tried to look busy, but like a kicker who just missed a game-winning field goal, no one was near him. He was getting the looks from the team, staff and crowd; looks like that of a loser.

"Let's go in with a two minute drill. No huddles, no substitutions." Bodie snapped. Coach Ramsey said nothing. He talked with coach Patterson upstairs, probably hearing the same advice.

"Marcus looks like he's bruised from head to toe." Ramsey used that as an excuse and it wasn't really far from the truth. "No two minute drill. Not yet. Mistakes are going to made. Let's not panic: we're only down by four. But, alright. We'll do some pistol. We'll get you away from that line, and you throw, Bodie. We'll start thrown'."

Fremont Union's drive stalled at mid-field and they punted. Bodie went in and Marcus sat out the series on the bench. Marcus didn't seem to mind. The play selection was pass-oriented, with Bodie flaring out and hitting targets of opportunity. Fremont was easy prey, still bunching up on the line, but they soon sobered up to the fact that Marcus was out and Bodie was passing. Bodie got them into the red-zone, at about the fourteen yard line and had a pass broken up on third down. Coach sent in Brett, not that a seven to six score was going change things much. But as a team is often reminded, a field goal isn't always a "gimmie." The Fremont Union defensive line smelled blood and came rampaging in early. They pounced on Brett when he was fully extended and blocked the kick. Flags came out from three different directions. Brett didn't get up. He lay in the fetal position, nursing his knee. With the off sides penalty it was still fourth down, but only fourth and one. The whole crowd shouted "Go. Go. Go." But instead Coach Ramsey sent in Hester.

"You're shitting me. You're shitting me, right?" lamented

Bodie. It was fourth and one, but it was a long yard. Too long for coach. Coach Ramsey could hear him, but he had been pretending not to hear him all night long. He let the comment go. It would be almost a 25 yard kick, thanks to the penalty. But everyone held their breath, knowing nothing was a 'given' tonight. CJ hiked the ball, Harrison held and placed it with a second of fumbling, and Hester kicked it. The ball hooked left, but sailed through the uprights just above the crossbar. The applause was deafening. You would have thought they had won the game. Hester and the kicking team came off the field. The momentum had definitely shifted. Fremont received the punt and was stuffed on every down. They punted, three and out.

Coach Ramsey kept up the passing attack, flooding zones, running deep post patterns. Fremont was now shell-shocked. They left big gaps in coverage not knowing if Marcus, who was in now, would run or if Bodie would throw. But they stiffened in the red-zone again, the drive stalling at the nineteen. It was third and four. Coach sent in still yet another running play, down the middle.

"No way. No freaking way." Chase had brought in the play to the huddle. He apologized for the limp play selection. Marcus looked scared. He knew he wouldn't drive it in four yards.

"Okay boys: he's just setting us up for another shakey field goal. Screw that. Marcus, halfback option. We all sweep right. "You run the mother wide but if you see someone open, don't be afraid to hit him. We've done this in practice every week. Let's do it. Ready? Break!"

CJ hiked the ball shotgun. Bodie handed off the ball to Marcus. He sprinted wide; the lighter line sweeping well with him. But before the line of scrimmage he saw Chase wave his arm as he had three strides on the cornerback. The corner just couldn't make up his mind on pass or run. Marcus planted his feet and passed to Chase. It was only fifteen yards, but everyone held their breath. Chase's soft hands pulled it in and he jogged in for an easy TD.

The place went crazy. After high-fiving Chase, Bodie ran into the bench area. After he took off his helmet he could see Coach staring at him, as if laser beams were going to emit from his deep set eyes and burn Bodie to a crisp. Coach Ramsey walked up to him and asked in a low voice, "What was that?"

But before Bodie could answer, Coach Ramsey marched off. For a few fleeting moments the crowd thought Ramsey was some kind of genius. Dressing down his quarterback would admit the game-winning play was not the one he had sent in. After time had expired they sang the school song at the bleachers and then hit the showers. The scoreboard had read 13 – 7, but as Bodie scrubbed the sweat off of his face and blew the blood out of his nose, he wondered if the team would win another game all season.

"Who ya voting for?" asked CJ, not being rhetorical. Chrissy and Bodie weren't laughing. The Homecoming dance was semi-formal, but they definitely didn't dress for it. Chrissy just wore a black skirt with a white blouse, something she would probably wear to work. Bodie wore a white shirt, black skinny tie and a pair of khakis. The tie was loose around his neck, but that was the same with most of the football players- out of necessity. Bodie looked up at CJ. His friend tonight, instead of looking like an un-made bed, was dressed in a dark suit with a red tie. And was that... styling gel?

"We voted for Chase, the Stanford man," replied Chrissy. "And Melissa Carter, cheerleader extraordinaire." Chrissy looked CJ up and down. "I would have voted for you if I saw how good you looked, slick." CJ blushed and toyed with his jacket button. "Think so, huh?" She had made his day.

The gym was a newer variety. The old one was torn down. It was decided they could go state-of-the-art for not much more than doing an earthquake retro-fit of the old one. The old one was getting too small anyway. The new one had a flat ceiling, unlike the airplane hanger arch of the old one. It had a built in stage for bands or school plays. An accordion wall could be opened to enlarge it for school dances and an area for drinks and, in some cases, food. The expansion area reminded him of the food court in the Mall. There were about twenty fixed tables and chairs, permanently mounted to the ground. When they had gone to the Mall Thursday night, they ate pizza on the same fixed seating, watching the people walk past. Bodie couldn't help but to zero in on a certain few. Coming to the Mall had always been the high point in his youth. When he got his drivers license, it became a frequent stop. The Altamont Renaissance Fashion Mall was an Italian street re-creation inside a cavernous set of promenades. Shops lined the walkways beneath high ceilings alternating with brass-lined skylights. It had two levels in certain areas, but at the food court the high ceilings created an open space that was almost overwhelming. Bodie decided he had now spent way too much time there, now that he could recognize some of the crowd, like some kind of Jane Goodall recognizing her chimps, giving them names.

Frequently, at night, a hideous figure might be seen on the delicate open-work balustrade which crowns the towers and runs round the apsis – it was still the Hunchback of Notre Dame. At such times, according to the reports of the gossips of the neighborhood, the whole church assumed a fantastic, supernatural, frightful aspect; eyes and mouths opened here and there; the dogs and the dragons and the griffins of stone which kept watch day and night, with outstretched neck and opened jaws, around the monstrous cathedral, were heard to bark and howl. The Hunchback of Notre Dame

"Earth to Bodie," whispered Chrissy. "What the hell are you thinking?"

CJ had wandered off, strutting his stuff, leaving them by themselves. "I'm really worried about my grades." Bodie reported, still staring off into the noisy gaggle of teenagers. The band had taken a break while the votes were being gathered. There would be an announcement any minute. In the meantime nearly 800 people tried to talk over each other. "I'm getting no press, no college has talked to me since Cal Poly came by during Hell Week. Man, they're only FCS. If my GPA goes further down, I'll have to sit out the rest of the season. I'll wind up hanging out at the Mall all day. Like those guys we kept seeing Thursday night." Bodie looked at Chrissy now, his eyes morose. "I can't do community college. But that's where I'm headed. JC football. What circle of hell is that?"

Chrissy ran her fingers through his thick hair. "I understand. Completely. I still have those incompletes from last year when I had that strep throat. I missed so much school, I'm not sure if I have the credits to graduate. Dean Horner called me in and says the only way I can graduate this year is if I take two JC courses. Their units are, like, triple ours."

Bodie sat up, surprised. "Babe, you didn't tell me..." His eyes were wide now. "That bad?"

Chrissy only frowned out of one side of her mouth. "Maybe I'll get a taste of River Island Community College," she said sternly. "I can let you know just which 'circle' it is!" They couldn't laugh, but they were smiling now, at least.

Out of nowhere, it seemed, appeared Dean Horner. He was well dressed, accompanied by his wife. He leaned over and put his hand on Bodie's shoulder. "Bodie, Coach Ramsey wants to see you in his office Sunday morning at eight o'clock sharp. Don't be late." He then strutted up to the stage. Chrissy leaned over. "Melissa says they're having marital problems. That's why he's so grouchy lately."

Suddenly a drum roll. The band was back. "May I have your attention please! It was Hector Rentería, wide receiver and impromptu emcee for the vote announcement. Jocko was next to him with a huge ballot box. "It is time to announce this year's King and Queen of Homecoming Night!" Behind them was Dean Horner, supervising. Hector and Jocko wore bad suits, Dean Horner a tux. The drum roll grew louder. Jocko turned the ballot box upside down, acting as if it weighed 80 pounds, out tumbled but one envelope. Hector opened it up. The crowd hushed, finally.

"This year's King is... Chase Bettencourt!" The crowd screamed.

"And his Queen will be... Melissa Carter! Melissa Carter! All right!"

Everyone clapped. Bodie and Chrissy stood up and clapped, still smiling. There was some relief, but oddly, some sadness.

"I'm sorry you guys," blurted Gena Rhodes. She was another cheerleader. She was sitting at the next table. She became a cheerleader only when Chrissy got sick and was out so long.

Bodie looked at Chrissy as they stood and clapped for the happy couple. "One less picture in the yearbook, I guess." There was a bit of dejection in his voice. He couldn't hide it. She looked back at him and smiled a sad, sad smile.

3
BLACK SUNDAY

BODIE WAS USED TO COMING INTO SCHOOL at all hours, all days. It was Sunday morning, eight o'clock sharp. But he wasn't looking forward to it. Coach Ramsey would have to be pissed at having his play substituted by Bodie on Friday night. He was going to hear about it this morning he guessed, without an audience. He jogged into the locker room to find that Coach was in his office with three older men. The office was enclosed on two sides with glass from waist high. Bodie had seen some of them at games, but had no idea who they were. They were large men, getting larger at the belly, late fifties he guessed. He knew at least one of them was active in the Booster Club. They had serious looks on their faces. They stood with their arms crossed while Coach Ramsey sat in his task chair. He seemed to nod a lot. One of them noticed Bodie standing near the lockers and looked at his watch. They filed out, one by one.

"Bodie! Bodie Houge. Good game Friday night. Good game." They smiled, patted him on the shoulder. They reminded him of used car salesmen. Coach Ramsey poked his head out of the door and motioned Bodie to come in.

"Hey Bodie. Sit down."

"Who were those guys?" asked Bodie, slowly settling into the other task chair.

"Oh, boosters. Friends of the Administration. Old football jocks..." Bodie could tell coach did not want to talk about their presence here today.

"Look: I had a long talk with Dean Horner and he's keeping an eye on all the athlete's GPA's. As you know we lost three guys to bad grades this quarter. The bad grades went back to last year. We gave them one quarter to get the GPA's up to 2.3-- the minimum required to participate in sports at Altamont High. Their fourth quarter grades didn't cut muster and they were cut from the team. Antoine Washington is getting his grades back up... he will probably get to play the rest of the season-- depending on how he fares on finals. Finals are week after next. You have got to get a couple of B's and no goddamned D's, Bodie. What happened to you? Grades weren't a problem in your Frosh 'n Soph years." Coach reclined in his task chair. "Lemme guess: Senioritis?"

Bodie began to squirm in his chair now.

"Bodie, you've got the hard stuff out of you way. No math. No Biology. And now you're having trouble in... typing? 'Come on man!"

"Coach... they should just make typing pass or fail, you know? I just can't let go. I over-think it."

"Dang-it, you kids grew up with computers. I figured you picked up typing on your own."

"I'm great at using a joystick. Point 'n click... no problem.

But I just always hunt and pecked when it came to typing. Not very fast. So I took typing, --er, Word Processing. Made sense at the time..."

"You got English. Typing. Sociology. History and ... Art. You're putting in the effort in Art.. a little more and you could probably pull an A. Why not? They thought you were doing well in English. Mrs. Krautman is going to talk to you after class tomorrow to see how you're progressing. You got a big book report due before finals, right?"

"Yup."

"I don't see any reason why you can't get at least a 2.8. That is more than enough to get you over a 2.3 average. You can do this Bodie. We can get you a tutor. Need one?"

"Coach. It's a lot of reading. Book reports, history." Bodie slowly shook his head. "That I can handle, but Sociology... I... I have to read each paragraph, like, three times sometimes to get it to sink in. I'm up to midnight most nights. It all adds up."

"Well, college is that amount of reading times five Bodie. Hunker down. No malls, no distractions. Okay?"

Bodie got up with the assistance of his hands pressing on his knees in one fluid motion. "All right. No malls."

"Oh. And Bodie: we're going to mix it up a little more, as Marcus is banged up a bit. We'll pass more often and I've got some new plays that we'll run through this week. Plus..." Coach threw Saturday's Chronicle sporting section on his desk in front of Bodie. On the front page, above the fold, was a big color photo of Hester on the sidelines. Her helmet was off; they must have taken it soon after she kicked the field goal. The players beside her were yelling and patting her on the back.

"The Boosters think we can put her to work. You know, she originally wanted the QB position. Don't worry, she throws okay, but she doesn't have a lot arm strength. I know she's just a Sophomore, but I am moving her up ahead of Harrison. He'll continue with field goal placement holding, but I'm getting pressure to play her. Not much. Don't worry. Situations..."

Bodie let it sink in. 'Say what...' He thought to himself. Was this some kind of head trip to get his academic ass in gear? "Look Bodie; when was the last time the Chronicle paid this much attention to the program? It's a big-assed article, too. We're on the map again. We've got Max Kolbe up this Friday and they are hot. They're on a streak. They don't win by much, but they've been finding a way each week to eek out a win. Those private schools are allowed to bring in out-of-district players, unlike us. They've got some African kid on defense that is really messing up league offenses. We'll see video this week on him. But they will have no film on Hester. Big surprise. But just..., you know, situational, okay?"

Bodie nodded. Coach Ramsey swatted his ass on the way out the door with the sports section.

As Bodie walked to his car, he couldn't get the image out of his head of the players around Hester. In the photo, he had seen himself sitting between two standing players, looking up at the commotion. If there was an in-depth article about the Altamont Highlanders, no one had asked him squat about anything.

It wasn't three hours since he told Coach Ramsey that he'd hunker down, and here Bodie was at the Altamont Renaissance Fashion Shops, eating a Philly Cheesesteak in the food court. He didn't exactly plan on it, but on the way out of the school parking lot he saw CJ and Jocko pulling weeds as punishment for throwing tinfoil balls at freshmen from the senior pit area. The seniors had their own area during lunch and breaks, including a four by eight foot Bar B Que pit surrounded by picnic tables and an actual lawn. Lower class men were forbidden to trespass on part of this sector, but invariably every September to October an unsuspecting freshman would wander into the 'Senior Pits' and get an atomic wedgie or be simply launched off the property. But Jocko and CJ couldn't leave well enough alone, and continued to pelt one freshman every time he walked by, for an infraction in early September. They were accused of bullying and had to pull weeds for three hours. They checked out and caught a ride with Bodie from school for lunch at the Mall.

Sunday was always busy in the Mall; crowded promenades, escalators, shops and the foodcourt. There were about 20 permanently mounted tables with chairs planted firmly into the concrete and tile floor. Across the main promenade was a mirror image of the food court with another 20 tables. On both sides the tables were surrounded by the usual fast food outlets, plus some one-of-a-kind local entrees. Toward the center of the mall were two levels of shops with extra stone finishing to make the interior truly Italian Renaissance-esque.

"How's your book report comin' along, Bodie?"

"Crud..., don't remind me. I'm still reading the book."

"Oooo," sighed Jocko, between mouthfuls of a calzone. "Mrs. Krautman isn't going to want to hear that. You have to give her a progress report so she can mark it the hell up and tell you what you're doing wrong. Mine was full red marks and corrections. But at least I had almost four pages done. Dude! Put something down, on paper, man. Can't Chrissy whip something up for you?"

"Naw. She's behind on a bunch of incompletes... I can't ask her to do that. She would, but it would really mess her up."

"What book are you reading, anyway?" asked CJ.

Bodie chewed his Philly cheese steak sandwhich and looked at the Mall. It's upper tier, its architecture, the giant free-standing clock at the center crux. It was odd that the clock protruded out of a planter of lush green plants and dwarf palm trees. It was mounted on a rectangular box and had a large round face of almost 15 feet. If you met someone at the mall, it was always at the clock. It was in the center, not far from the theatres. Bodie never got tired of looking at the clock, with all of its arms pointing to dates and months and astrological symbols. What amount of precise gears mounted on a bushing or a jeweled stylus must be inside of it! In addition to all the symbols were figurines. People of the Renaissance. One looked like a portrait of Dante that he had seen in his history book. But on the far right was a skeleton, standing ominously, looking down. "What the hell is up with that?" He wondered.

Someday they would open the last expansion wing of the mall, but for now it was an odd, flat dead end with no brickwork or tile, just a flat brown paint on temporary plywood. A space of 30 feet separated it from the clock. Once open, it would create the last arm of a four spoke axis that would be the Altamont Renaissance Fashion Mall fine.

"The Hunchback of Notre Dame," Bodie droned. "Its nothing like the cartoon."

Jocko chuckled with his mouth half open with food. "Everybody knows you don't read the Disney books. Movies. Cartoons. The teachers hate 'em all!"

"I know! I know! I got Victor Hugo's version. It has to be. It's so fricken' hard to read. It's in 'olden day English. It's like

Shakespeare talk. It's hard to read. I have to re-read it all the time. It's taking forever... There's a whole bunch of people that weren't in the movie or the cartoon. I can't fake it man."

It was obvious no one wanted to talk about it any further. Bodie was just plain screwed.

Bodie saw a guy walk by that just plain hung out at the Mall in perpetuity. He swallowed the last bite of his cheese steak.

"That guy..." pondered Bodie, half dreamedly. "He is here all the time."

"Mall Dweller," defined CJ. "There's a bunch of them that hang out here. I think he went to Altamont, like, four years ago."

Without making eye contact with his friends, Bodie kept watching the 'Dweller.' "Is this where you wind up when you don't get accepted to college?"

"Well, most guys get a job. Then they hang out at the Mall," explained CJ, suddenly professorial. A chill ran up the back of Bodie's legs, then darting into his bowels. 'Holy shit: that's me in eleven months,' thought Bodie with a shudder. The reality of becoming an NFL Quarterback was suddenly just a pipe dream. Now he had little chance of even finishing his high school senior season. This certain Mall Dweller was haunting him now. He was the measure of complete and utter failure.

"Oh, the ugly ape!" cried one.
"And as mischievous as ugly," said another. "'Tis
the Devil himself!" exclaimed a third.
"I am so unlucky to live near Notre Dame, and hear him

at night prowling about in the gutters."

"What! with the cats?"

"He is always on the roofs."

"The other night he came and grinned at me through my garret window. I thought it was a man. I was dreadfully frightened."

"I am sure he attends witches' sabbaths. He once left a broom on my leads."
"Oh, the ugly hunchback!"   The Hunchback of Notre Dame

"Bodie, what did coach tell you?" asked Jocko, genuinely concerned.

"Just to get my grades up. And that..."

"And what?"

"He and some old geezers from the Booster Club wanna see Hester get more playing time."

"So? Harrison is out. Big deal."

"He wants her to Quarterback in 'situations,'" sneered Bodie, making quotation marks with his index and middle fingers.

"No way. No way!" CJ and Jocko were thunderstruck. Bodie could only shrug his wide shoulders. He knew they wanted an expanded explanation, but Bodie just didn't have one.

"Boys, as the old saying goes, the world is doing its best imitation of a frozen yogurt machine as it shits all over me. That's it in a nutshell. I'm getting it from all sides. I guess I'll just take what I can get."

4
THE NOOSE TIGHTENS

"BODIE, I NEED TO SEE YOU AFTER CLASS." Mrs. Krautman injected as the bell-tone buzzed. He was already standing and ready to bolt to lunch. He closed his eyes and walked zombie-like to her desk. The class schedule constantly rotated, each class getting closer to being the first morning class, then disappearing for a day. Today English was before lunch. Mrs. Krautman had him for as long as she wanted.

Mrs. Krautman was forty-something. Bodie could tell she was once a looker, back in college perhaps. She still wore her hair long. It was brunette but now with gray streaks in it. She was going natural. She had no wrinkles yet, but her eyes looked tired, always. Bodie decided it was from grading papers deep into the night, no doubt. But then when she talked to him, there was an intense fire deep inside those eyes. He thought it must be from some strain of DNA that made English professors be English professors, one that trickled down from the middle ages and drove them to insert some kernel of wisdom from the 'Classics' into the fertile young minds of the twenty first century. Whatever it was, she had it, and there would be no pussyfooting around it. He would understand the book, and write a dissertation on it proving that those kernels of life-lessons and wisdom were deeply imbibed in his teenage brain.

"Well, you know your grade is floating in the 'C' range right about now, Bodie. You do the work, do okay on the tests, turn in the work... but with just a little effort you could be flirting with a B+ / A-.''

"Yes m'am. Dean Horner mentioned something like that. In other classes, too."

"How's your paper coming along? You didn't hand in a progress report..." Bodie could tell she didn't think he had squat. He slowly pulled out four pages of an eight page book report. Yes, he had stayed up until two last night doing it. Surprisingly, his newly acquired typing skills made it two instead of three-thirty. She took the paper. It was neat, freshly laser printed. She began reading it right away. Her red pen came out. It darted here and there. But there were long pauses. Even entire paragraphs went unmarked.

"Good Bodie. Good. At least you have clued in on the fact that the book isn't about a disfigured man running about Paris. It's a class study... yes... this isn't bad. At least I can tell you're reading the damned thing."

"It is a hard read. He writes like olden day talk."

"Like a mountain climber, you acclimate to it... you get used to it." She put it back on her desk and looked at Bodie. "Look, Bodie; I'll give you the report back after school. Come and pick it up. Study for the vocabulary tests-- there's only two left plus the final. Hand in the book report. I'll even let you hand it in the day of the final; that's a couple extra days. Do good on the final and the vocab' and this report might put you way over a B. Maybe even the A. You're that close, Bodie. Okay?"

"Yeah. Yeah. I can do that."

"Just a little bit of focusing and you can nail this class Bodie."

Bodie got up. "Thanks Mrs. Krautman."

"Bodie...," Mrs. Krautman patted his report that lay on her desk. "This is good."

He didn't realize it at first, but as he walked out onto the Senior pit to join Chrissy, he felt good about himself for the first time in weeks.

After a brief stint at the public library, Chrissy and Bodie settled into the food court at the Mall. Some malls may be dying in America, but the Renaissance Fashion Mall seemed to have what it takes to keep people of all ages coming in. Bodie thought that The Italian Renaissance theme mixed with 21st century flooring, lighting and skylights. They seemed, at first, a little odd, but somehow it worked aesthetically.

Thus the Roman abbey and the philosophical church, Gothic art and Saxon art, the heavy round pillar, which reminds you of Gregory VII, papal unity and schism, St. Germain des Pres, and St. Jacques de la Boucherie-- are all blended, combined, amalgamated in Notre Dame. This central mother-church is a sort of chimera among the ancient churches of Paris; it has the head of one, the limbs of another, the trunk of a third, and something of them all. --The Hunchback of Notre Dame

The Oh Max! Theatre near the south end of the mall would bring people in at all hours. This would keep most of the food court eateries open when most of the shops had closed. Even the large anchor stores like Stacys and Mears would be closed along with one of the axis spokes, but the cattle trail from the theatres to the main entrance just so happened to be strattled by the food court. Bodie watched the late night movie goers leaving the Mall. Mixed among them was the Mall Dweller he kept seeing. What movie did he watch tonight, wondered Bodie.

Chrissy had been talking with Melissa, who was working tonight at 'Bad Dog', a hot dog / corn dog / hamburger eatery. Bodie continued to watch the small crowd file out. A few stopped in at the food court. Strangely, the Mall Dweller turned and looked over his shoulder, looking at Bodie as if he knew someone was watching him.

Melissa and Chrissy clued in on Bodie staring off into oblivion. Chrissy looked at Bodie. "Yoo hoo... Mr. Quarterback..."

"Chrissy, if I wind up a mall dweller, will you kill me, please?" Bodie was still watching the Mall Dweller as he wandered away into the night.

"Kind of drastic, wouldn't you say?"

Melissa zeroed in on whom Bodie was starring at. "Oh that Mall Dweller. You do see him around. One time I was in the catacombs dumping some garbage and he was skulking around. He scared me at first, but then he walked out a service exit."

"Catacombs?" Bodie asked, a little incredulously.

"Yeah, that's what the mall crews call them. They kind of smell. The garbage from cookie eateries and milkshakes melting and all the pukey stuff parents can't get their kids to eat winds up stinking up the catacombs so bad that it never leaves, even after garbage pick up. If you wander around far enough, there's an administration office on the second level that's all lit up and bright. The windows look down on this intersection of catacombs... to keep an eye on things I guess. It's where the Mall security checks in and accountants work who come out and harass the local store owners for their rent. Gena used to work at Abernathy and French. She said she went in there one time after a shoplifter ran out with a $400 dress. They have this room with a bunch of monitor screens. It's scary how much they can watch you here. They tracked the shoplifter to the parking garage and nailed her."

Bodie's attention drifted to a large screen TV inside of Holy Grail Pizza Pub. Something bad had happened. He couldn't hear the news, but there was a commotion in a forest. A shaky news camera was showing a wrecked truck and a medi-vac helicopter. He wanted to get closer, but minors weren't allowed in the Pub section .

"Oh man, now what?"

"I think it's those eco-terrorists again... up in the Sierras."

Bodie and the whole world was getting tired of the eco-terrorists who where sabotaging forest harvesting projects in a variety of ways, sometimes resulting in lumberjack deaths. "They hit something big this time." Bodie looked at the time on his cell phone. "Crap. It's late. Let me take you home."

"It's no big deal. My parents like you."

"No. It's me. My dad is getting on me about staying out late now that my grades are dragging. Dean Horner talked to him on the phone yesterday."

They marched outside. It was autumn and the Delta Breeze hit them in the face. The main Mall entrance faced west, catching the cool wind head on.

After dropping off Chrissy Bodie came in through the front door juggling books and a laptop. He put them down on the kitchen table and noticed someone was still up, watching TV.

"Still up, Dad?" There was late news still running. Footage of the logging truck was running again.

"Yeah. I'm about to call it a night." Bodie's dad still had on a work shirt. He worked at the giant wind farm on the Altamont. The Delta Breezes channeled through the flats of the San Joaquin Delta and the surrounding hills to power thousands of high tech windmills, cranking out megawatts of electricity.

"Those god dammed hippie kids are at it again. They torched a bridge up in the Sierras and a logging truck fell through." The wreck was spectacular. There were a few passenger cars in the collapse, as well.

"The trucker had 45,000 pounds of logs crush him to a pulp." He shook his head. The news reporter blamed Hetch 22, a eco-terrorist group who claimed credit for the act. Among other things, Hetch 22 wanted the dam at the Hetch Hetchy reservoir removed so that the valley, which rivals Yosemite, could live again. The main problem was the entire San Francisco Peninsula relied heavily on the reservoir water. It was, in fact, the sole source for water for the city of San Francisco. They were now leaving demands and threats on You Tube. Their posts usually starred their leader, a man in a ski mask called Commander Plastique. Bodie had watched some of their demands at the senior pit on other people's I Pads. "That guy is nuts."

Mr. Houge struggled to get out of his recliner, newspaper

in tow. "Of course he is. All of his trail mix eating conspirators and hairy arm pitted girlfriends are just trouble. Just plain trouble." Bodie could still hear him mumbling something down the hallway, but he couldn't quite make it out. He liked his dad, but he was a bit of a grouchy bear. From down the hallway snuck his younger sister Katy. She was in eighth grade and actually anxious to get into high school.

"I thought he would never go to bed. I think he was waiting up for you, asshole." She switched channels to a late night showing of "The Paper Chase." She had been watching it on her old, small, cathode ray tube TV in her bedroom. Although it was about Law School, something Bodie couldn't care less about, he began to relate to the desperation of the characters and their need for good grades. Katy loved the idea of going to high school and college. She was an active, athletic girl with brunette hair and had the physique of a volleyball player. Her volleyball skills might land her a full ride scholarship someday. Bodie was amazed at the devotion and focus of these law students. Was it really like that in college? A young Lindsey Wagner kept his attention.

The next morning Bodie got out of the shower early and dressed. He looked at his room. He heard Katy walking down the hall and stuck his neck out his bedroom door. "Hey. Can I have your dry erase board? You don't ever use it."

"Sure. All yours." She was just happy to have the bathroom to herself early this Tuesday morning. He retrieved it from her room. It had been on the floor, leaning against the wall since it had been sacrificed to make room for a Radiohead poster. He hung it on his wall and wrote a five day calender, one for Monday and then each day of finals, Tuesday through Friday. As an afterthought, he edged in atop of Friday, 'Charter Stockton.' They would still have two league games after the Charter Stockton game, but everyone knew Friday would be for the league championship. Bodie lightly chewed on the end of the marker. He was going to focus on this week. Focus, focus, focus. Just like "The Paper Chase" when two of the characters holed themselves up in a hotel room and crammed for finals only in their underwear. He gave each day the name of one of Quasimoto's Bells:

[MONDAY] THIBAULT

(reg. classday)History

Bodie arrived to the Bar B Que Senior Pit and it was lunchtime and he was ready to eat his lunch. CJ came up with the Chronicle. "Hey guess who's above the fold..."

Chrissy turned from Gena and Melissa to see what was in the paper. It was Hester Sargeant again featuring some kind of player profile, as though she was the new starting quarterback.

"Daaaaaaaaaaaaang..." CJ just couldn't contain himself. Jocko and Hector walked up to see what the big deal was. "Coach talked to me about this..." They all looked at him at once. "Like I said before, he's going to play her in 'situations', okay?"

"Yeah, sure... okay." There was no argument, but this was wrong. Just plain wrong.

"What's your next class, Bodie?" asked Chrissy. "Typing?"

"Yup." Bodie was grateful for the ending of silence. "Look: Coach wants me to give her some pointers on the Quarterback position. Big Deal. The papers picked up on that.

Or Coach clued them in on it. Either way, it's just Hester getting ready for next year. That's all, okay?" Bodie chomped on his tuna sandwich. With that, Chrissy, Melissa and Gena headed to class.

Bodie finished his sandwich and crumpled his empty lunch bag slowly as he watched Jocko and Hector harass another poor freshman for wandering too far into the senior pit lawn. He walked over and took Jocko's powerful arm off of the hapless freshman's neck. "Run along, and be free young one." With that, Bodie gave the Freshman a gentle shove to get him on his way.

"What was that? Jocko asked incredulously. Jocko and Hector could see Bodie was bummed out on the way the season was unfolding, and the stress of class testing.

"Meet us by the dumpster, by the biology lab." They walked away quickly.

Bodie could tell they were up to something. The biology lab was near the edge of school bordered by a utility access road. The garbage was picked up there, at the dumpster. The dumpster was enclosed by a brick wall with wooden swing doors. Because of its remoteness, the dumpsters on the south end of the school were hangouts for smoochers, smokers and students sunning themselves. With lunch only half over, Bodie found Jocko and Hector drinking out of a fast-food paper cup. When they saw Bodie they pulled out a mason jar from the side of the dumpster. It had orange juice and ice cubes swirling around in it.

"Here man; fifty cc's of stress release."

Bodie took it, sniffed it and drank a long, long drink. He grimaced for a second and uttered, "Any orange juice with your vodka?" They chuckled. They took turns gulping down the forbidden drink. Usually Bodie didn't take chances like this, but he was exasperated and just plain hated typing class. The warning buzzer blew. They had two minutes to get to class.

"Here. You finish it 'bud.'" Jocko handed Bodie the paper cup.

After killing the drink, he tossed the paper cup into the dumpster. "Jocko, you're smart."

"Huh?"

"You got all your hard classes out of the way and now you're just cruising through... getting good grades."

"Hey. Drama is not an easy class." Then Jocko burst out laughing. He was getting an A. He had a knack for hamming it up in front of an audience and so did Hector. They also both had typing class and they did well in it. It seemed to come to them naturally.

"Here chew this." He gave Bodie some gum made by a nature company as they walked to typing class. It was supposed to really cover up the alcohol. Bodie wasn't going to trust it, but he put it in his mouth anyway, thinking it might help a little.

Typing class was actually called 'Word Processing'. It was a basic class, but this late in the quarter it was getting more and more complex, and the words-per-minute quotas were getting higher. But instead of being stressed out, Bodie was relaxed as he settled into his work station. He had a Devil-may-care attitude as he put in his personal CD.

Mr. Parks, the typing/business instructor, was a square. He was a younger guy that had his hair cut short and was full of nerdy cliches.

"All right class. Settle in. Get with the program. We're doing a proficiency test right away. Let's go." Bodie began typing from a sheet of copy on his stand. The entire class was clicking away on their soft keyboard keys. But something strange was happening. Bodie was gliding right along. He suddenly wasn't the caveman stomping down on his keyboard. He was relaxed. He wasn't double checking everything. He wasn't making errors. Somehow the half jar of Screwdriver mix was giving him permission to just execute. He was in the Zone. The only time he felt like this was when he was in a close game, the ball was hiked and he was dropping back and scanning the field for receivers. Time wasn't moving, only he was. There was no attention paid to sound, wind, smell... just touch. But at the same time he had a heightened sense of vibration; footsteps, bodies hitting the ground and even the friction of the ball in the air as the threads cut against it during rotation. Whatever that was, it was happening here in typing/word processing.

Mr. Parks was lurking behind him. He could tell. He now had eyes in the back of his head. Just like when he was in the pocket and a linebacker was hooking in from outside, from his blindside, he could perceive Mr. Parks gaping at his proficiency today. He was cool with that. It was okay. He was in the Zone.

A white square timer bleated on Mr. Parks' desk. It had an amber light that flickered in unison with the audio signal. It didn't really matter though. Bodie had typed the entire sheet of the exercise. Very few of the class ever did that.

"Outstanding Mr. Houge. How'd you accomplish that?

"This is a big week for me, Mr. Parks," replied Bodie, making eye contact but keping his breath down and away from his instructor. "I'm just trying to focus and concentrate on everything.

Mr. Parks patted Bodie's shoulder as he walked past. The printer up front ran off everyone's typed sheet. Jocko beamed at Bodie and contained an explosive laugh. He had to. The electronic bell hummed as Jocko and Bodie walked out to their next classes.

"You did great man."

"Yeah, I guess I did." admitted Bodie

"You got Art Next?" Asked Jocko as he veered off.

"Yeah. Doing more silkscreen."

"Man, you've got nothing to worry about. Your grades will take care of themselves. I've got Drama. Talk about an easy 'A'." Jocko waved his hand and jogged down the open air hallway.

The Art room was just a few doors down from the word processing room. The Art class was loosely structured, but you had to put in the work. Projects had to be completed and there was a quality control issue. 'Effort' was considered, but it would not carry you. Dan Cofield was the instructor. An easy going guy of thirty one, everyone got along with Dan. No one messed around in Art though. It just wasn't cool. This was Bodie's first inkling of what college must be like. Dan was slender, had longer feathered back hair like he was from the seventies. He had a long skinny nose that matched his fingers. He reminded Bodie of a bird. Flamingo?

Robotically, Bodie got out a silkscreen that already had a stencil made. He had taken his time on carving out the stencil. It was for his lunchtime volleyball team in the spring. The whole school had teams slung together and played a bracket. The winners played a faculty team just before school got out. He looked forward to it every year. He knew enough jocks to have a great team every time.

Dan came by as Bodie started silkscreening the first color of his two color T shirts.

"These will be great, if you can pull them off." Said Dan as he surveyed the first shirts. "Can you get these to register?"

"Yeah. I'm just going to let them really dry. And I made some registration blocks." Bodie knodded to some two by fours nailed to some plywood. He would just have to push the silkscreen of the other color into the blocks to get the second color to line up.

"It should be close enough."Agreed Dan.

"Dan, do you think I can pull off an 'A'? I don't know if they talk about struggling football players in the faculty lounge, but I could really use one this quarter."

Dan's focus remained on the Volleyball jersey. "We talk about a lot of things... look: do a good job on these and do something, anything for extra credit and you will get the 'A'. How about that tapestry you were thinking about. You silkscreen that and you'll get the 'A'. Hmm?"

Bodie at one point was going to do a medieval tapestry using some black light ink. Mostly unicorns, prancing goats and fleur de lys on a dark navy blue sheet. Maybe it was the influence of the Hunchback of Notre Dame. He just thought it would look cool under a black light lamp he had over an old Pink Floyd Live poster.

"Yeah. I can do that, yeah." Dan moved along inspecting other projects, giving encouragement.

'Maybe Jocko was right, Maybe I can do this.' CJ stuck his chubby neck over Bodie's shoulder.   "'The Blitz'. Alright! I can't wait for Volleyball lunchtime action! You have my size, right?"

Bodie melted into his desk in Sociology class. This is where reality was going to rear its ugly head into Bodie's life again. He stayed up late typing his English book report at the expense of reading his Sociology chapters. Bodie refused to believe three and four chapters a night was approved by any high school governing body. If you had two or three of these kind of classes, you could never keep up with the reading. It could theoretically add up to nine chapters almost every night. Someone was screwing with the workload limit and it was Mr. Hagan.

As class dragged on, Bodie thought he could actually avoid any questions. Mr. Hagan began reviewing another chapter, this one on ephemeral groups. The only reason Bodie took this elective class was because Chase was taking it. In fact, he chose all of his electives based on which football players were taking what. But he forgot that Chase was the intellectual, the soon-to-be-Stanford man.

As Mr. Hagan wrote on the big dry erase board, Bodie looked at Chase with a little desperation.

"'Read the chapter?'"

Bodie shook his head. "I didn't read any of them. I was still reading last week's when I started my book report."

"That's not good. Mr. Hagan can spot a bullshitter from a mile away."

Mr. Hagan looked as though he was a retired general. He was a big guy with hair slicked way back; always wore a sport jacket and tie. He was about as no-nonsense as they came. He was about sixty.

"Ephemeral groups." He announced. What can you tell me about them, Bodie?" Bodie cringed. The jig was up. "Well..., ephemeral groups are people that are associated by a common interest or pursuit, like for instance a nature group, lets say. Maybe like the Hetch 22 guys. They all have a..."

"Didn't read the chapter, Bodie?" Mr. Hagan glared at Bodie with his hands at his hips. He had had it. "What Mr. Houge missed out on was that these groups are, in fact, quite the opposite of formal associations or... 'clubs'..., they are spontaneous amalgamations of people that meet quite by chance, and sometimes do not even interact with each other. It could be people waiting for the crosswalk signal to change to green. Transitory. People in an elevator. Or, at other times people that can't stand the heat during a long, hot summer and just mingle outside at night trying to stay cool during a power black out. But sometimes these groups do interact. They may get together to solve a problem. Like an assembly of angry parents at the front door of a school administrator when the grades of their children hit miserably low levels." Mr. Hagan scowled at Bodie.

"Or they may demand changes during that power black out and go on some kind of riot. These groups are mostly temporary and benign, but sometimes... volatile. Any spark can make them explode. It may take a million factors, but sometimes most of those factors are already there, latent, waiting invisibly. Turn to page 172 in your textbooks and you can see that they site three examples...

Bodie was beyond caring. 'Screw this', he thought. Bodie somehow knew this was a class better suited for a semester format. It was a six pound course in a five pound bag. Mentally he and Mr. Hagan had just written each other off. Bodie was on his own. Mr. Hagen wasn't even going to waste his time on this jock with after school tutoring or an after class chew-out.

He would just reel out all the rope Bodie needed to hang himself. Bodie looked at Chase, who was, of course taking notes. Chase looked up. Bodie flipped the bird at Mr. Hagan as he began writing on the board again.

Coach Patterson and Bodie watched Hester take snaps from under center, in this case, C.J.. Bodie wondered if C.J. might be getting a little bit of a thrill from having a nice looking girl put her hands so close to his 'scrote.

"Okay Hester, good, but it's okay to put some weight on your back foot. And then just shift it forward as you throw... a good fluid motion... it will put more umph on your pass. Okay?"

Coach Patterson gave Hester a pat on the pads and jogged over to the receiving corps. Bodie was to give her kernels of QB wisdom the best that he could.

"Here's Chase Bettencourt, the most productive wide receiver on the team. He brings his own ladder to the game and gets the high passes no one else can," beamed Bodie, as Chase jogged up.

"Hey."

"I've watched you two link up dozens of times. You're going to Stanford, right?" Asked Hester.

"Yup. You know your stuff."

"I like to think so, but now I'm finding out how much I don't know..."

They heard a tweet of a whistle. Coach Ramsey motioned for someone to come over. "Hester! Come on!" Coach Ramsey was next to Brett who was on crutches. It was Brett's turn to give Hester pointers. This time on the kicking game.

"Chase, what's going on?" Bodie really wanted to know.

"With Coach Ramsey?"

"Yeah. The whole thing. The play selection. The boosters, and now Hester. She's a nice chick and all, but why all the falling over backwards to take a sophomore like her on? It's more than just equal sports for girls. There's more going on here, man."

Chase nodded his head. "Those boosters..., they pull a lot of weight. Not just the money they pull in for football; they have a lot of connections. Coach Parsons, from last year? He's at Cal now because of Sellars, the big booster. He used to play at Cal. He's a member of all those service clubs and they all get drunk together and go to the big conventions. A real 'Player'."

"So they all just rub elbows and do favors for each other, huh?"

"Just call it networking. If he can get the 'rep for being a scout for Pac 12 teams, and he keeps delivering, they keep listening. He's considered a resource."

"You know him? Sellars?"

"I do now. Bodie, I didn't know it at the time, but he's the one that got Stanford interested in me. Those guys he sits with in the stands aren't always some member of the Rotary Club or the Moose... sometimes they're coaches and scouts. That's why I don't want you to quit with your schoolwork, man. If they were looking at me, they were looking at you. They talk. If they don't need a QB they wind up talking to a desperate head coach at Podunk U. that is all ears for an unsigned high school QB that everyone else just didn't have room for. I know you gotta be on their radar. I just know it, man."

Bodie knew Chase wasn't just making this up to boost his flagging ego. There just might be hope still. "Thanks, Chase. My other classes aren't as bad as Hagan's. No where as bad. I might pull it out. It's just all in the finals, man."

"Good. There's two games left after Charter Stockton, and they'll take us to the CIF. You're the only one that can take us. Not Hester, not Harrison; you. If your GPA sinks under the accumulative 2.3, you'll miss the boat... and then we all miss the big dance."

Hetch Hetchy before the dam.

Hetch Hetchy after the dam.

5
THE FICKLE FIELD

VS. MAXIMILIAN KOLBE HIGH

"Listen up lady and gentlemen! I think I made it abundantly clear that Max Kolbe doesn't have to play by the league rules..., that is, they can recruit outside of the district... way out of the district. In this case they are playing Dominic Konare. He's from... ah, coach Patterson; what shit hole is he from anyway?

"Uhh uhh, ... Upper Volta, I think." replied coach Patterson, suddenly upbeat. "Someplace in the darkest of the dark continent. Hell, I don't know, but some missionary from the Catholic Church could tell he could be some kind of middle linebacker, that's for sure. They sent him state side and he's been kick'n ass ever since, that's for sure."

"Okay. We've been all look'n at Kunta Kinte for three days now and we know he could be playing at any division FBS college school right now, right away. Maybe even be a starter. Two hundred twenty pounds and six- two. Nothing fools this guy. He seems to be blitzing when he wants. Staying home when it's necessary. Their coach lets him call it any way he wants. He's not dumb. He leads the conference in tackles, sacks and hurries. Okay. Okay. Now we're going to sling his sorry ass. Everything is shotgun tonight. We're going to speed it up. If he blitzes, fine. He'll be late. No sacks, some hurries. This is where a rushing attack and a passing attack help each other out. Hester is going to get some playing time because they have no film on her. She has Quarterback skills that could help us out in situations. But don't worry; Bodie's our man. We're just going to keep them off balance. No last minute film. Let's just go out and kick some Crusader butt! What's going on here!"

"Highlander football!" Everyone ran out of the locker room like crazy men. They were not going to over-think this one. The band played extra loud and the crowd was into it. There was only one more home game this season, so everyone was going to make the most of this one.

There was a slight rain sprinkling against Bodie's face. It rarely rained this early in the year, but a tropical storm was breaking up over southern California and its remnants were dropping on Highlander Field. 'The football gods takin' another whiz in Bodie's Wheaties,' he thought to himself. He was paging through the playbook. It wasn't supposed to be on the field, but Bodie thought he could find something that could work. The coaches agreed he could make calls on the field, but sparingly. There wasn't much in the book to choose from. Coach Ramsey had gutted it, for some reason, and now they were trailing Max Kolbe 20 to 10.

"How are the ribs?" asked Coach Ramsey.

"Fine Coach, they're fine. I just got crunched a bit, but I'm fine."

"Okay, I'm taking Harrison out. Do some warm-ups and I'll send you in."

Bodie had gotten blind sided by Dominic Konare in the third quarter and by the time he was done grinding him into the turf, he had a hard time getting up. Bodie never felt this before. Bruised ribs? Cracked ribs? He wasn't sure, all he knew was that it hurt every time he took a breath. He looked around to see if anyone noticed him grimacing. Someone was next to him.

"What does Coach have in mind?" It was Hester. She was warming up as well.

"I have no idea, except Harrison is moving us in inches."

There was a collective 'ooooooooooooooooooh' from the stands and a thud from the field. Harrison got sacked on third down by Mr. Konare. The punting team went in along with Hester. Harrison hobbled off the field with one arm over CJ's neck.

"Bodie: can you go back in?" asked CJ tersely.

"Yeah. Next series. You okay, Harrison?" Harrison only grimaced. He remained in a half-hunch. Coach Ramsey walked up to check on Harrison. He only watched the trainers probe his ribs.

"Ahhhhhhh!" was all Harrison could muster.

"Coach, the playbook is still so thin this season. We... we need more selection, man."

"We've talked about this before Bodie. It ain't the play selection. It's the execution. When we had too many plays, this team was getting all confused in hell week. I had had it man. You saw Harrison out there. I think knowing what was in there got him through two series."

"We didn't score. It didn't work. We need more."

"Ya think so?"

"Hester. Hester!" Hester had just punted a 29 yarder. Max Kolbe was threatening again.

"You go in next series. Warm up!"

Bodie could see her gulp from where he stood. He walked back to the bench to read the play book again, but just looked at the logo on his helmet instead. It was simply a coat-of-arms style decal, with two crossed Scottish broadswords and a shield with a green plaid pattern and the Scottish thistle centered on it. Some thought it had the look of a private academy. Bodie always thought that there was something special about his high school. Did every kid think that? He watched Hester warming up. He had nothing to tell her. Coach Ramsey was having a tantrum, so Bodie was going to let him enjoy it.

Suddenly the crowd cheered. They had had nothing to cheer about tonight. Hector had just intercepted the Max Kolbe quarterback (again). Time was now becoming a factor.

Hester started out with hand offs to Marcus and a new sophomore. Dominic Konare was a little off his game, but began blitzing, trying to get into the backfield before they could set anything up. Bodie had warned Hester about this and she ducked an attacking Kanare with her short stature as he skidded past at an angle. The hole he left in the backfield left Hector wide open. She hit him in stride for a forty yard pass and run. As the officials ran to set the ball, she read a laminated play list on her forearm. No huddle- her idea, but still Coach Ramsey's plays. She stepped back, barking out the count. CJ hiked the ball and began blocking with all the extra effort he could muster. No one on the line wanted to let Hester get her ribs crunched tonight. She found Chase just a step in front of a defensive back. Both her passes were only fifteen yards, but the yards-after-catch were mind blowing. Chase scored. The kicking team went out. CJ and Jocko came in, out of breath. The 110% effort they were giving for Hester was taking its toll. Hester kicked the extra point and now it was suddenly 20-17. Time was running out.

The defense took the field with extra urgency. The momentum had visibly changed. Max Kolbe had to get two or three first downs to keep the ball from Altamont and win this game. But the best way to lose a game was to get conservative and that's exactly what Max Kolbe's offense was doing. Their running game was not their strength and the Altamont 'D' was not going to give up any yardage easily. Max Kolbe went three-and-out.

Coach Ramsey sent Hester out again. He didn't want to mess with the rhythm now. Again they mixed the pass with the running game. It was making Dominic Konare hesitate for a second, but in football a moment's hesitation can buy you a completion, even a touchdown.

On first down Hester dropped back to pass. Dominic anticipated this and ran straight through the offensive line, timing it perfectly. He fell on Hester, the ball popping out as she hit the ground. It was ruled a dead ball. Dominic knew they had to stop Altamont here. This would be Hester's maximum field goal range. He was not going to let this game go into overtime. The Highlanders all had their hands on their hips as they slowly walked to the huddle. They were breathing hard; the 110% was petering out. They were now having trouble punching open holes for Marcus. Hester thought some wide outs could get the ball out of the pocket in time before any Kanare threat. But in two tries, they only gained three yards. It was now fourth and a long ten and seven seconds on the clock. The Coach sent in the field goal team. She worked it out in her head that it would be about a 34 yard attempt, which she had only done in practice once.

Harrison knelt down to place the ball after the snap. Hester peeked at the crowd on both sides of the stadium. They were all on their feet. She measured her steps backward and CJ snapped the ball. It was so quiet she could hear birds outside of the stadium. It was a perfect snap, as usual. Harrison reached out to plant the ball, but it slipped through his hands. He tried to snare it back, but stopped-- his ribs cried out. The ball began hopping out to Hester's right. She tried to scoop in the fickle orb, but it was wicked, so wicked. As she got close she could feel heavy hoof beats behind her. Using the eyes in the back of her head, she veered away from the tide of the defensive line as soon as she snagged the ball. Her short stature allowed her to zig as the big hosses zagged en masse right past her. She darted out to the left side which had no one of either team around. She thought of running, but she knew she didn't have the speed to reach the goal line, not from this distance. She glanced at the scoreboard; there was no time on the clock. There were hysterical screams erupting from the stands on both sides. Below the scoreboard she saw a lone figure jogging through a pass pattern. He wasn't even looking at her. It was Ted Studemire. Bodie never used him. He was too slow and had stone hands. He was essentially a decoy in every game, that is, when he was in. She planted her feet; she was dangerously close to the line of scrimmage. *'Look over here you big dummy...'*

As if he had heard, he looked right at her as he began ending his jog/post pattern. He realized it was coming his way, and began finishing his route. He now had to catch up to it. He straddled the goal line as he caught up to the soft pass. He made a half hop and brought it in. Six points. The Highlander stands went nuts. The Highlanders were five and two.

There was a short dog pile on Ted, but Chase brought it to the side line before the officials threw a flag. A sloppy kicking team tacked on the extra point. Everyone gravitated to the stands and sang the school song. Hester was the center of attention, getting hugs and kisses on the cheek. Bodie was happy too. But he glanced over and saw the Kolbe Crusaders on their side of the field, slowly gathering for their school song. It was obvious this one hurt. They were not a powerful team, but their finesse and dogged tenacity allowed them to eek out a win every week. But not this evening. After the Highlander song was over, Bodie looked at Chase and nodded his head toward the Crusaders. They walked over carrying their helmets and tried to sing their song. The opposing quarterback and Dominic Kanare saw them and put an arm around them. Bodie had heard their school song many times, but this time it was slow, sorrowful; almost a dirge. Their coach nodded at them. By the time the song was over, a dozen Highlanders had come over. They shook hands, said "good game," and called it a night.

6
THE GAUNTLET

MONDAY COULD BE LOOKED TO AS A DAY of preparation for finals, but Bodie had spent all day Sunday studying for History, English, and even Sociology. He was now even optimistic of his finals. He had caught up on his Sociology reading, sans last week's burden, and was feeling good about his History class final. And Hector was to be trusted on supplying his magic juice for Friday's Typing/Word Processing final. It wouldn't be clear sailing, he thought, but he was armed and operational. Monday was his last day of regular classes, but some classes would fall in between his finals. Usually they amounted to study halls. But some sadistic teachers continued class study, as in Ms. Krautman's case, reading scholastic periodicals out loud. But, as always, Sociology brought Bodie Houge back to reality.

Mr. Hagan kept the heat up on Bodie for some reason. Bodie was able to respond to his reading questions, but Bodie began to feel a little shell-shocked. Was his final going to be one of those nebulous written tests that you couldn't figure out what the test was asking, let alone what the answer was? Bodie thought if he could just carry a 'C' on the final he could get the 'C' for a semester grade.

At the Senior Pits Chrissy gave encouragement to Bodie for a good week in finals. Gena was there offering one of her usual snide comments.

"Why the worry? They find a way to pass the jocks anyway, right?" she said, in all seriousness.

"Gena..., now days, it's about the opposite. They are riding Bodie big time." Chrissy said in a lecturing tone. "All this state testing and minimum standards stuff is making it really hard. They aren't messing around anymore."

"Okay, okay." Gena said, getting up from the picnic table. "Bodie will do fine. Typing and English. Come on..." She gathered her books and walked away.

"I beginning to hate that bitch," rattled Chrissy. "She weaseled in on my cheerleading spot and didn't offer to give it back. No wonder she doesn't have a boyfriend."

Bodie looked surprised. "Rearrrrrrrrrrrrrrrr," he sneered, using his forefinger and middle finger to form quotation marks... or paws.

"Yeah. Yeah, you got that right. I heard she was in a certain someone's backseat Friday night. Everyone knows."

"Nothing gets by you. Dang." whistled Bodie.

"No." Chrissy got up and grabbed her backpack. "Meet me by the clock in the mall at five and I'll tell some really juicy stuff about your patron saint, Chase. Ciao, baby."

'Huh...?'

The rest of the day went by fairly well, but Bodie canceled any meeting at the clock. He had work to do. There was always reading. If there was really that much reading in college, Bodie began to shudder. It was a lot. He did it, but it took perseverance and he didn't have a whole lot of it. This week was probably going to determine the rest of his life, but the life-saving adrenaline and verve that usually kicks in at life-saving circumstances just didn't appear. He closed his books and put the finishing touches on his book report of 'The Hunchback of Notre Dame.'

Thibault

Mr. Beckman was a predictable guy. There were no surprises on his History final. There were some essay questions, and Bodie asked just what Mr. Beckman wanted to know on one about the politics of Bismark on Luxembourg. After a while Mr. Beckman made it clear Bodie was on his own. This slowed him down, but Bodie could smell a 'C'.

Jacqueline

After turning in his book report, the entire class took a final, mostly vocabulary. There were looks of relief on everyone's face, more so on Bodie's. Could he get the 'A'? He wondered.

Bodie tried to read more chapters for Sociology in the other classes that were in 'study hall' mode, but it was slow and difficult. Finally school was over and he headed to football practice.

Coach Patterson was looking at some history of football books while everyone was suiting up.

"What's that Coach?" asked Chase, as he laced his cleats.

"Oh, the old days. Old coaches, old plays, old formations..." Coach Patterson didn't even look up, he was just paging through it. It was more like a magazine than a book.

"What the hell is that?" asked Chase pointing at a formation of running men in leather helmets.

"The Flying Wedge. They outlawed it after it was killing people a little too much." The photo was taken from above, showing five players running down field with their arms interlocked.

"I guess a leather helmet didn't do much good against the Flying Wedge," responded Brett, to a small crowd of players, now dressed. They peeked over the assistant coach's shoulder for a peek at this dangerous thing.

"No, a leather helmet wasn't much good against it, especially when these guys hooked their fingers into their belt loops. It was devastating when it hit a kicking team. Dead players. I'm not joking."

"Come on coach, let's use it against Charter Stockton Friday night."

"Yeah. Fly'n Wedge. Come on coach." They began to chant.

"No, no, no. It killed people then, it'll kill people now. All right men, get the hell out there. We've got a lot to cover. A lot to go through. Coach Ramsey is waiting on you guys. Get on out!"

Gabrielle

A lot of people had already finished their silkscreen projects, but Bodie was silk screening his medieval tapestries for the extra credit. A small gathering watched as the last color of black light ink was registered and screened on the fabric posters. Melissa took off her top in the back room and asked if Bodie could put all three colors on her white 'T'. He agreed, and then, one by one, five of the other girls in class went in the back room and sent out their tops. Mr. Cofield, as cool and as hip as he was, was starting to get a little nervous about half the girls in his class huddling in the back room of his art department basically topless. All the guys were trying to act cool, but in reality they were dying to figure out an excuse to go in the back and look for parent sheets of paper or to pull out an old silkscreen. Mr. Cofield began to rapidly help Bodie lay out the shirts and laid down the first color.

"Gee. Thanks Dan," said Bodie, showing no indication of pressure.

"Jill! Get out the blow dryer," barked Dan, picking up the pace now, eyes riveted to the warm T shirts. "Alright Bodie, put on the last color right now. I don't care if the inks mix. Just get 'em done."

"But will it affect my extra credit if they do?"

"Damn your eyes, just get 'em done. Get those girls dressed, damn it!"

In the back room, Bodie could hear giggles over the drone of the cheap blow dryer.

On the Senior Pits, CJ and Bodie were reading the school paper, 'The Thistle.' There wasn't so much on the upcoming game with Charter Stockton than was the fact it was an anniversary of the Big Rumble when everyone got bent out of shape over the playing of 'Gimmie Shelter' by the Charter Stockton Commodore Marching Band.

"That's it? A history lesson? No sports?" lamented CJ,

looking for a story someplace else in the paper. "Yup. That's all. We'll have to wait for Friday's paper." 'The Thistle' ran Monday, Thursday and Friday, albeit Friday was the big issue. Bodie wondered if he could get above the fold in his own school newspaper.

Big Mary

It was quiet in Mr. Hagan's Sociology classroom as the students filed in. Bodie could even hear the impact of tennis shoes as their friction made soft noises on the tile floor. No one spoke. Not even Mr. Hagan. It was a long test, many short multiple choices. About a third of it was in one paragraph essay questions. Some of them asked about concepts Bodie just didn't recall hearing about in class. They must have come from one of the nine chapters that he hadn't read.

Hector was to meet Bodie out by the dumpsters for some go-go juice to get Bodie's typing words-per-minute up. But as Bodie neared the corner near the end of the school block, he saw Dean Horner hauling Hector around the corner, still barking at him. Dean Horner held the jar in his hand. At the spur of the moment, Bodie darted into the boys restroom, before Dean Horner caught sight of him. He spun around a dividing wall and listened to Horner yell at Hector. As he looked forward a small group of Freshmen were staring at him wide-eyed. They were smoking and realized it was Horner wailing outside. They scrambled into the toilet stalls and flushed their cigarettes. They began to file out, in case the Dean came in and smelled their smoke.

The last one said, "Hey man; I'm Cory. You saved me from some Seniors that were going to give me a wedgie or something Monday. I just... wanted to say thanks. I didn't have the chance then."

Bodie still had one eye on the door, half expecting Dean Horner to barge in with Hector held by the scruff of his neck. "Umm, don't mention it."

Bodie then cautiously slithered his way to his Word Processing final. Everyone was settling in as the tone buzzed, but Bodie's mind was on the final. He wasn't loose, and if the the go-go juice was some kind of placebo, he knew just by not having it, it would mess with his mind and his confidence. 'Please, no zingers!' he thought to himself. 'No tabs or weird columns!'

"All right everybody: get with the program!" Mr. Parks began to hand out what was to be typed on a xeroxed sheet as Hector trotted into class with a tardy note from the Dean. "Settle in Mr. Renteria-- 'got your note, I trust?"

Bodie noted that Mr. Parks was about 30 or 32. Did he have a romantic bone in body? He wasn't married. He wasn't bad looking but he cut his blonde hair short and combed it with water or something. He looked like an accountant or some kind of bean counter for the IRS. Not much of a sense of humor, either. Bodie finally got his copy of the test. "Oh man, tabs up the ass!" His shoulders dropped, his breath, his very life force exited his body. This was it. Even if he got a 'C' for the quarter, his GPA wasn't going to make up the deficit from last quarter and average out to a 2.3. He was dead man walking.

Mr. Parks grabbed his timer and pushed the button. "Begin."

There was no practice that day; they had a home game that night. The game. Charter Stockton. It would most probably be Bodie's last game as a starting quarterback. Last game ever. He decided it would be his CIF Sector

Championship, his swan song... his Super Bowl. He wasn't going to cry or moan before the game. No asking for pity. He just decided he was going to win this game; beg, borrow, cheat or steal.

7
A SHELTER OF ECHOS

BODIE DIDN'T EVEN BOTHER GOING HOME that afternoon. He called his parents to see if they were going to the game (they weren't), grabbed some fast food and suited up early. When CJ showed up, they practiced taking snaps. Other players showed up early for this one. This one was important.

"How are the ribs?" CJ asked.

"Better than Harrison's. I figure his are cracked."

"Hester going to play tonight?"
"Yup."

"Start?"

"No fricking way."

"That's the spirit."

"All right everybody: get inside!" Barked Coach Patterson. "Coach Ramsey is ready for you."

"Okay, okay simmer down lady and gentlemen." Coach Ramsey hurried in the stragglers as he began his pep talk. "Okay, big game. Big defensive line. The Commodores have a good quarterback. Reminds me of someone we know. But who cares? Big deal. We did a number on Max Kolbe last week; we can do another on these guys. They have their weaknesses, we just have to hurry things up to exploit them. We'll keep them off base. Substitutions, we'll play Hester here and there... Marcus is back in form... we'll do okay. But this one will be won in the fourth quarter. We might get behind, but we are not going to get blown out. Not in our house. It might go to OT. But at the end of the night, we can come out on top if we don't give up. Not for a second. We don't give up. I don't want to see anyone sitting on their helmets... hell, I don't want to see anyone sitting down tonight. We're going to be in a dogfight and it'll be us bite'n ass. What's going on here!"

"Highlander Football!" With that the team began to stampede toward the door, but then awkwardly studder-stepped to allow Hester to run out first. Bodie smiled at CJ and just shook his head.

The tie score at halftime started to melt away. After 17 all, Charter Stockton began to make adjustments, and really put on the pressure when Coach Ramsey sent in Hester. She just didn't have any time to read defenses and find receivers. Bodie hadn't fared too much better. But he always had his safety valves. Hector, who was made to sit out the first half in a deal hammered out by Dean Horner and Coach Ramsey, was in now. He was cold and had dropped two passes already. Bodie was even passing to Ted Studemire, trying to make things happen. But now they were down by ten points again, in the fourth quarter, just like last week. The whistle blew. The third quarter just ended. They began to walk to the side of the field for water.

"You okay, Jocko?" asked Bodie.

"I'm fine." Jocko was breathing hard. So was CJ, hands on hips. "That's about the biggest line I've seen in two years. "Can't believe they didn't start last year..."

"Jocko: remember your drama class?" asked Bodie. "Let's put it to use."

"Huh?" Jocko was guzzling some Gatorade, but came up for air. "How so?"

"When the big DT guy isn't looking, when the refs ain't lookn', you haul out and punch him in the gut as hard as you can. Then when he hits back, you act like you're out cold or rollin' on the turf like poor, poor, pitiful you. We can't let this drive stall, man. Do it. Do it on this drive. The refs won't see you but they'll hear the rukus and see him hit back. You play the victim. Can you do that, drama queen?"

Jocko drank more Gatorade but kept his eye on Bodie. "Yeah. I can do that. You're a bad man, Mr. Houge." Trainers snatched the bottles and ran back to the sidelines.

Bodie threw a short pass on second down. It was now third and four yards to go. Jocko heard one ref talk about a clock discrepancy to another. The side judges looked at each other and then at the scoreboard. Jocko hit the DT while even he was looking at the scoreboard. It may have been too much of a surprise as the DT was more stunned than hurt. By the time he hit Jocko in the helmet's faceguard, all eyes were on them. Jocko stepped backward like a drunken sailor and fell on his back, holding his jaw as if it was hit. Instead of getting back up and starting a fight, he rolled to his left and laid down. Jocko peeked out of his right eye and saw one yellow flag after another sail past him at the DT. Everyone was yelling, but Bodie pointed his finger at the DT and made a good case for sucker punch. But the damage was done. There would be no question and answer period. There never is when a punch is clearly seen. Whether there was trash talk or a shove to start it all, the refs didn't care. They just knew punishment had to be swift and final.

"Unsportsmanlike conduct. Defense, number 92. Player is disqualified." The ref pointed to the tunnel. Disqualified meant off the field, not even on the bench, not even on the sidelines. He had made a fist and threw it; Bodie knew it was all over but the shouting and started the huddle right away. It was an automatic first down and the goal line was a scant 21 yards away. Jocko walked to the sidelines for a few downs.

"Okay guys, while they're still rattled: Let's do that pass-shovel-tip coach never wants us to use. On three; ready--break!" The Charter Stockton line was eager, but already one step behind. CJ hiked the ball and Bodie faded right. Hector ran down field trailing Chase about two yards. As the safety and cornerback zeroed in on Chase, he went up high and caught a 15 yard pass. But before he landed, before he was hit by the defensive backs, he shoveled the ball at Hector, who was in full stride. By the time the defensive backs untangled themselves from Chase, Hector was leaping over the goal line. Charter Stockton stood shocked and aimless. Their coach was on the sideline, yelling at someone, but no one could hear him over the crowd. The Highlander band played as loud as it could. The overflow crowd was deafening. The stadium could seat about 3,500. But Bodie noticed the crowd had just kept growing, even past half-time. People were standing outside the end zones. He had figured they were listening on their car radios, and decided to buy their way in while the game was close. No one favored the Highlanders in tonight's game. But here they were, in the fourth quarter trailing 27 – 23. On the sideline coach Ramsey held up two fingers. They were going for a two point conversion. They weren't going to tie this one for overtime; they were going to win it in regulation.

Bodie could see Hester running back to the side lines but she had the look of happiness and anticipation. She was just fine with no kicking the extra point. The whole bench and coaching staff kept each other off of the field.

Coach Ramsey signaled an option run on the right side. Bodie ran a few steps, pitched it to Marcus. Marcus ran with the green sophomore wide to the corner, but instead of pitching it away, he kept it and ran over a cornerback to break the plane of the end zone.

"Who says Marcus can't run anybody over?" Bodie laughed. CJ smacked Bodie's helmet. The scoreboard read 27-25 with 4:11 left to play. No one doubted they could pull this one off. Bodie ran off the field and the kicking team took over. It was a good kick. They were playing toward the western end zone this half, but it was okay; there was no wind factor. Hester's kick went over 32 yards, a personal best, and wasn't returned, thanks to a motivated coverage team. Bodie stood on the sidelines with a wet towel draped over his head. Every eye in the stadium was on Charter Stockton's offense, which was paying for every inch. Every eye except for Bodie's. His eyes caught sight of the wind sock on the upper corner of the bleachers. There were short streamers on top of the field goal posts as well. He thought he saw a flutter. Then... there! There it was again! Bodie shut his eyes. The football gods were going piss in his Wheaties yet once again. The Delta Breeze, vacant all week, had reared it's ugly head. He looked over his shoulder up at the Altamont. The small windmills were spinning. But now the huge ones were rotating. Slowly at first, but now with authority. Their blades were over 100 feet long and they didn't start churning for nothing. A sinister marine layer off of San Francisco was causing cold air to be sucked into the hot valley via the San Joaquin River Delta. And if this game came down to a field goal, Hester would have to kick into the Delta Breeze. She had been improving, but she couldn't compete with that. Bodie leaned over and looked at coach Patterson, who caught his eye. Bodie looked at the streamers and then back at coach. Bodie could see the dim, vacant expression in his eyes turn to pupil-dialating panic. Coach Patterson immediately pointed it out to coach Ramsey.

One minute and forty six seconds remained in this game when Charter Stockton punted the ball away on fourth down. The Highlanders made a fair catch at their own twenty-nine yard line. You could feel the momentum change yet again in the stadium. Yeah, the Highlanders had the ball, but the Commodores defense had a 'come and get it-- if you can' attitude. Bodie began using coach Ramsey's plays. Bodie had done his part, but he wasn't going to stick his neck out on the final stretch... it was above his pay grade.

After a few sweeps with Marcus and an incomplete, Bodie followed orders and hit Chase on a post pattern; his bread and butter. The Highlanders were on the Commodore's forty yard line and everyone knew all that they needed was a field goal to win it. To no one's surprise, Ramsey wanted Marcus to run it up the middle. He tried to squirt between the new guard, who was much smaller, and the nose guard. He gained only two. They tried it again, but again for only two measly yards. It was third down, Coach Ramsey singled a crossing pattern for a first down. Bodie set up in a shotgun formation and CJ hiked the ball. Bodie didn't waste any time and hit Hector for a first down. As the ref set the ball, Bodie saw there was only twelve seconds left in the game.

"Chase: no time. Take it at the right hash mark five yards out and let's hope Hester can nail it."

As soon as the ref set the ball CJ wasted no time getting set.

"Rathole six! Rathole six! Hut!"

The Commodores were barely ready for action. Chase ran east/west behind the defensive line and Bodie hit him in stride. Chase abruptly turned up field and actually made it to first-down territory with four seconds left on the clock. As they moved the chains Coach Ramsey called time out. Bodie veered by Hester as she ran on field. "You can do it girlfriend!"

A nervous smile broke out on her face as she trotted to the forming huddle.

"Ted, how long does it have to be?"

Ted was already scanning the field. "About 36 yards … maybe a little more."

"Crap. That's her limit. And the breeze. The god damned breeze, man."

"Then pray. Just pray," said Ted, completely exasperated.

There were waves of screams and random whistles, but only in hand fulls. The whistle blew and CJ hiked the ball. This time Harrison planted it perfectly and Hester kicked it with all the form of an NFL starter. The thud of her cleat sinking into the ball echoed through the stadium. It was off. Bodie studied the streamers atop the field goal posts. They were fluttering. Not strong, but fluttering. The ball had less of an arc than her usual kicks, but she knew she would have to flatten it out to make the distance and not let too much air get under it during the up-wind flight. It cleared the defensive line, just barely. It was true enough, slightly to the left but within the margin for error. After it sailed 36 yards, it hit the crossbar and bounced back toward the goal line. The refs signaled 'no good'.

The entire sideline was stunned. Time had expired. The

opposite side of the field erupted in cheers. The Defensive line for Charter Stockton picked themselves off the turf, but they weren't celebrating. For a brief moment they had thought they had lost the game. They just collected themselves and walked back to their sideline. But their sideline was jumping and hollaring all over the place. The band began to play.

Hester had taken off her helmet and fell to her knees. She just sat there. Bodie walked out and knelt with her. He didn't try to pick her up. Coach Ramsey could see he was consoling her, coaxing her to come back to the sideline. Finally, she stood up, with the back of her hand to her eyes, her head down. By the time they reached the side line the Highlander band was playing the school song. No one was trying to leave and beat the traffic. Most gravitated to the band and the team at the 30 yard line. But before they finished, the Commodore Marching Band began playing again. This time much louder.

Bodie saw some of the sophomores of the team break off and start running to the other side of the field.

Then some fans came piling out of the bleachers.

"What the hell?'" Bodie thought to himself, turning around. But then it dawned on him: the Charter Stockton Marching Band was playing 'Gimmie Shelter' on his field! That was not cool. And over the end of their school song. Bodie found himself jogging over to the Commodore Band. No one was really thinking what what they were doing, they were just reacting. Just mad.

"Hey! Shut up. Shut the hell up you tuba-playing pussies!'" A large group of players veered toward the 50 yard line where the Football Commodores were entering a tunnel beneath the bleachers. Jocko was at the front of this spearhead. He began throwing punches around. A couple of linebackers came at him, but were knocked down right away. He was pissed, frustrated and really didn't like playing the victim during the game, even if it gave them a badly needed first down. Some of the Commodores' coaching staff were calling back some of the team out of the tunnel. "Get back here you guys!"

The band played on.

Chase and CJ were trying to grasp the situation. Small groups were still trickling out of the bleachers onto the field. More and more football players ran toward the Commodore bench where Jocko was. Coach Ramsey, sensing a riot, ran after them to stop them. "Where's Bodie?" screeched Chase.

"There— by the band!" CJ was pointed toward the main body of the band, somewhere near the twenty yard line. They could see Bodie, but he was going down in a circle of band members, throwing punches.

"They'll kill him!" Chase surmised as they ran full tilt toward the melee.

Chase realized three other players were running with CJ and himself. Most of the Commodore Band was clustered around Bodie; they appeared to be cheering or jeering whatever fight was going on inside.

"Flying Wedge! Flying Wedge!" ordered Chase. In a flash, all five players, some still with their helmets on, interlocked their arms as tight as they could while maintaining a sprinter's pace. Some of the band somehow sensed the oncoming mad bull about to shatter their formation. They peeled off just a second before the flying wedge smashed into the human circle.

Quasimoto observed the confusion of the rabble, the consternation of some, and the alarm of the stoutest; and at the sight of this unexpected succor, he mustered strength enough to throw down the foremost of the

Trumpets and trombones flung about helter skelter. Most of the band was still playing 'Gimmie Shelter'; the resulting crash rendered the musical notes YAH, YOO and BONK. The band was mowed down like some kind of formation of dominoes. This caused a shift in the attention of the visitor stands. People started to come over from the mid field bleachers to the odd crunches and toots coming from the band.

"Where is he? Where is he?" bleated Chase, almost in a panic. CJ surveyed the mob like a faithful sheepdog.

"There! Right there!" Bodie was on his knees over a poor bastard, wrapping a trombone around the band member's neck, like some kind of brass necktie. Other members of the band were trying to pull Bodie off, but he would have no part of it.

Quasimoto, with heaving bosom, watched the movement of the great bell Big Mary. The first shock of the clapper against the wall of brass shook the wood-work upon which it was hung. Quasimodo vibrated with the bell. "Vah!" he would cry, with a burst of idiot laughter. Meanwhile the motion of the bell was accelerated, and as the angle which it described became more and more obtuse, the eye of Quasimodo glistened and shone out with more phosphoric light. Quasimodo placed himself before this open mouth; he crouched down and rose up, as the bell swung to and fro, inhaled its boisterous breath, and looked by turns at the abyss two hundred feet deep below him, and at the enormous tongue of brass which came ever and anon to bellow in his ear. All at once the frenzy of the bell would seize him; his look became wild; he would watch the rocking engine, as a spider watches a fly and suddenly leap upon it. Then, suspended over the abyss, carried to and fro in the formidable oscillation of the bell, he seized the brazen monster by the earlets, strained it with his knees, spurred it with his heels, and with the whole weight and force of his body increased the fury of the peal. While the tower began to quake he would shout and grind his teeth, his red hair bristled up, his breast heaved and puffed like the bellows of a forge, his eye flashed fire, and the monstrous bell neighed breathless under him. It was then no longer the bell of Notre Dame and Quasimoto: it was a dream, a whirlwind, a tempest, vertigo astride of uproar; a spirit clinging to a winged monster; a strange centaur, half man, half bell; a species of horrible Astolpho, carried off by a prodigious hippogriff of living brass.

Hunchback of Notre Dame

"Bodie! Bodie!" screamed Chase.

Bodie turned his head as he pressed and pressed the brass necktie tighter and tighter around the band member's neck, as an emergency tech gives CPR to an accident victim. His eyes were crazed; maniacal. He looked right at Chase, but there was no look of recognition. He continued 'tying' on the necktie.

"Bodie! We have to get outta here! You're attracting attention!" pleaded Chase.

"This is one hell of an ephemeral group!" Bodie cracked, still pressing the 'necktie'.

Chase looked over his shoulder at the people reaching the edge of the bleachers. They were looking at their smart phones, switching on the video apps. Without direction, CJ grabbed one of Bodie's elbows; Chase followed suit. In robot fashion,

Bodie braced his elbows and was lifted away, knees still kneeling. They carried him instinctively under the bleachers. CJ reached down with his free arm and snagged a marching band hat with a fluffy plume. Chase looked at him with an incredulous frown.

"Souvenir." retorted CJ.

"Bodie-- if they started video on you, it would have been all over. No CIF. No Big Dance," said Chase with a sense of urgency. "Without you the team goes nowhere. And they will punish people for this."

"Yeah." Agreed CJ as he huffed and carried his share of Bodie. "Heads will roll, man."

Standing in front of them was the lone figure of Ted Studemire. Standing as derelict as his pass routes, Ted motioned the trio over to himself, underneath the bleachers.

"They open this gate for overflow crowds to exit. And there's definitely one in the house tonight! Come on!"

With that, Bodie came out of his stupor. He planted his feet on the ground as they weaved through the bleacher struts and beams. "We can't go walking through Altamont in our uniforms and cleats, you guys."

CJ and Chase froze. They were just thinking on how to get out of the stadium unseen. They hadn't thought that far ahead. "It's okay you guys." Ted was pointing to the parking lot outside of the visitor bleachers. It served all of the spectators parking. "I brought my mom's mini van. She has a hide-a-key wired to the front end. I can drive us."

"Man, what happened to your face?" Asked Ted as he spied Bodie's eye socket.

"Someone in the band hit me with the open end of his trombone while I was punching out his friend." Bodie touched the cheekbone and eye socket of his face plate. It was swelling now. It probably did look bad.

A crusty older security guard walked up, not liking the hurried pace of the football refugees. "What's going on here?" he asked, shining a flashlight in their faces.

"Highlander Football!" They roared in unison. They marched on without hesitation.

Ted crawled under the fender well of the mini van. After some scratching noises he popped up with a black box. He pulled out the key as he hurried to the driver's door. Chase slid open the large side door and the other three piled into the back, hunched over.

"Get us the hell out of here, Ted," said Bodie in a whisper. "You can take us to my house. My dad will be cool about this. He'll understand."

Ted rolled down his window as he cautiously slipped out the driveway of the stadium lot. He could still hear screams and an occasional trumpet. Altamont police cars began streaming in, followed by San Joaquin County Sheriff Department Deputies. Three police vans accompanied them.

"Good timing, Ted. Good man," said Bodie as he peeked over his windowsill.

Mr. Houge answered the door with the newspaper in his left hand. He figured it would be Bodie at this hour of the night. Katy leaned around a corner to see if it was, in fact, his older brother.

"Evening boys. Come on in." Mr. Houge left the door

wide open. Bodie and his friends tip toed in as if they were naked. Bodie intended to go straight to the hallway and into his bedroom when his dad bellowed. "What the hell went on tonight? It's all over the Channel 8 news."

They all froze and then stepped closer to the large screen TV, mesmerized. They saw isolated images of police with billy clubs hitting people almost at random, trying to restore order. Always in any shot people were running in front of the camera. And in the distance more people ran in various directions. Some looked scared, some looked like they were having fun. Some looked as if they were running for their very lives.

Katy turned to the Oakland channel. It was on there, too. She switched again to the Sacramento stations. It was all over each station with more angles of the same bedlam. One Sacramento channel had shots from a helicopter.

"They were playing 'Gimmie Shelter' on our field, Mr. Houge. They knew it wasn't cool to play that song in our house and they did it anyway," replied CJ. "The band was beat'n on Bodie and we just dragged him outta there and split, as fast as we could."

Mr. Houge looked at Bodie's eye. He squinted as he examined his face. "That's going to be a shiner. What did they hit you with, anyway?"

Bodie hung his head and sat down. "A trombone."

Mr. Houge was obviously angry. Then a smile cracked on his leathery face. His work on the windmill farm left him exposed to the elements, especially the sun.

"A trombone, huh?" He began to laugh. The rest of them smiled. Then they began to laugh, too.

"Why is it always the trombone guy that can't get it right?" They began to howl and it broke the ice. For once, Bodie and his friends didn't feel like they were in any kind of trouble. It was an absurd engagement. There was no other way to resolve it.

"Did you hit him back?"

"Yes sir, oh yes." Mr. Houge slapped Bodie on the back and went into the kitchen. He emerged with a six pack of Sierra Nevada Beer. He handed them out to the boys, kept two for himself. They laughed some more. CJ pointed out a great punch by someone in a Highlander uniform, then they all shouted when another slammed his helmet onto a drum major. The neighbors next door, if not yet asleep, must have thought they were watching a boxing match on TV. Bodie could feel the pain in his cheek and eye fade away due to the swelling and the alcohol. He looked around seeing his friends laughing and yukking it up with his dad. CJ was now wearing his 'souvenir.' Bodie knew this would be one of those life long memories that he would treasure forever. It just might have been the first happy moment since summer.

8
THE COLD, BONY
FINGER OF SHAME

"BODIE. BODIE! WAKE UP. It's coach Ramsey on the phone. Bodie!" barked Bodie's dad.

"Huh? What time is it?" moaned Bodie, still half asleep.

"It's eight-fifteen. Pick it up!"

"Hello?" Bodie said fumbling his land line.

"Bodie; Coach Ramsey. The League Office has called a board of inquiry for twelve noon at the school gym. I need you to bring in CJ and the receivers, okay? We have to round up most of the team. You gotta be there. The shit has hit the fan on this one."

"What's the big deal?"

"What happened last night was all over the news... now its on the morning national news! Have you seen You Tube? Someone posted the worst of it and its going viral. More people are posting what they videoed on their phones. The League is in full fire control now. They have to. They need to cover their asses. Mr. Sellars says the Governor himself is on their ass."

"Umm... yeah... I'll be there."

"Bodie: be there with your guys at eleven. I think the whole city is going to be there. Get there early. I'll see ya." With that, an immediate 'click' terminated the call. It sounded like Coach Ramsey had a thousand others to make.

Bodie took a quick shower and jogged down the hallway. His mother had a bowl of cereal waiting for him. Mr. Houge had Bodie's cell phone by the bowl. In between mouth fulls, Bodie called CJ, Hector, Ted, Chase and a couple of other players. They all saw the morning cable network news organization channels and it was what everyone was talking about.

"This isn't happening," Bodie said out loud, after making his last call. "Everyone has a ride. CJ and Chase will ride with me. He cringed when he saw a drum major hit a football player with a baton.

"I'll drive." Mr. Houge ordered.

"Huh?"

"I'm not going to miss this." Mr. Houge was standing, finishing a cup of coffee. "Besides I want to talk to you guys on the way there."

"About what?"

"Bodie, I can smell an ass-covering from a mile away. The League has some explaining to do. And it is always done with a scapegoat. Someone is going to be assigned the blame. That's how these things work."

"Really?" Bodie wondered. He began to get nervous.

"Let's go."

Mr. Houge and Bodie had collected CJ, Ted and Chase. They all reported some of the You Tube postings. It was about fifteen minutes to the High School.

"Yeah, Bodie...," began CJ, "one of the postings you could see a band member walking around all zombie-like with his trombone around his neck."

"Yeah?" replied Bodie, with a nervous laugh.

"Look you guys; I don't how guilty you are, but one thing is for certain: you have to have the same story." Mr. Houge had the sound of a guy who had 'been there.'

"You have to be on the same page. No one has interviewed you yet. But the first thing cops do is separate you, get your stories, and see how the stories differ," explained Mr. Houge. "That's how they can tell someone's lying. And just who the liar is."

They all looked at each other. They began to repeat the night's events, through innocent eyes and convenient memories. It all just 'happened.'

"Your best bet," Mr. Hough counseled, "is to just say someone shoved you and then you shoved back and then...well, all hell broke lose. You don't even remember who threw the first punch. That kind of thing."

"Okay, Dad. You think they will even ask?"

"It all depends what they have on camera. You think you

saw everything? On the News, on You Tube? Don't bet on it. There's always a Zapruder film that pops up. You'll see."

They all eyed each other. "A Zebarooter what?" asked a bewildered CJ.

They could tell by the parking lot that this event would 'sell out.' Inside the gym a set of banquet tables were set upon the main stage next to a large screen jumbo tron. No one was sitting down just yet on the stage, but men in suits were milling about, talking to the Principal. Along with Channel 8, every news team from the San Francisco bay area was there, along with all of the Sacramento stations. With still one hour to go, the gym was over half full.

Coach Patterson approached Bodie with a swift step and a serious face. "We have a few rows reserved up front for you guys. Better hurry, they're filling up."

"Bodie I'll sit back here. It'll be all right," said Mr. Houge.

"Dad..." Bodie looked lost.

"Yeah. I know. They made it a big thing. Don't worry. These things blow over." Mr. Houge looked at Bodie and knew he was worried. "Bodie, these things always produce a scapegoat. I will wager they've already decided on one. But it isn't you. Don't ask me how I know, but I do. It won't be you. You're the good guy. Besides, you look like a victim." With that he slapped him on the shoulder and walked back to the regular seating.

The League Panel seated itself and actually banged a gavel.

"They actually brought a gavel. They must mean business," Bodie thought to himself.

"Order. Let's have order..." Said the League

Commissioner. "Order please. This hearing by the Delta-Crest Conference is in session. This is a diagnostic inquiry relating to the events of last night. We are not going to go any further afield than just getting to the bottom of last night's... disturbance. Cause and effect. This, ladies and gentlemen, can not happen again. We will hear from a very short list of witnesses and render a decision Tuesday noon on remedial action and, if need be, punishment."

Bodie could hear cameras that still used auto shutters and their servos. He didn't want to look behind him. The ambient noise of a thousand voices rose and fell behind him. People were still coming in. He felt like a prisoner waiting for the guillotine. He looked cautiously to his right at CJ. The kid was spellbound, as if he was at a Star Wars movie. Bodie looked to his left. Chase sat composed, concerned.

"Chase; if..." stammered Bodie, looking down at the floor. "If I've screwed up your Stanford scholarship... please forgive me. My ass is grass. I can live with that. I've made my bed and now I have to sleep in it. I can deal with that. But if you miss out on Stanford because of what I've done... I can't live with that. I could never make it up to you. Not in a million years, man."

Chase broke a small, knowing smile. "Let's just see. I don't think they're good enough. They don't have the goods. Not on us. We got away. No one saw our numbers... just be cool, stick with the story." It was a silly conversation, with both of them looking down as they spoke.

"Jocko, on the other hand; his ass really is grass," warned Chase. He was right. Jocko was all over You Tube swinging at other football players, yelling at the Charter Stockton coaching staff, front and center. Right at the fifty yard line.

"The Board of Inquiry calls Giocomo Tognazzi, Altamont High School."

Jocko walked up to a bare-bones podium. A small microphone was attached, nothing else. He made small steps-- he just didn't want to be there. He wore a nice white polo shirt with khaki slacks, his hair wet and combed.

"Please show cut 31." The Commissioner/Chairman requested. The place went quiet. The lights were dimmed to about 20%. For a moment, there wasn't any sound accompanying the video. Then it kicked in, hoarse and distorted. It echoed in the large gymnasium. The video showed Jocko and two other players, already at the Charter Stockton sideline. Their helmets were off, Jocko was yelling something. Charter Stockton players were turning around from their trek underneath the bleachers to the visitor locker room. But then it became obvious Jocko wasn't yelling at them, he was yelling at the coaching staff. Some of the Commodores came back and tried to put a distance between Jocko and their coach. One of the commodores shoved Jocko and and then he began swinging. The image was coarse, slightly under lit, and, because of movement, blurry.

"Cuts 36 and 37, please." It was more of the same, but from other cell phones at slightly different angles. After some time, the other Highlanders began throwing punches, too. But just before the end of cut 37 something was apparent.

"Can you freeze that, can you please?" The other members craned their necks to see exactly what he was zeroing in on.

"Now I want you to pay attention to Coach Banks, the assistant Coach of the Commodores... go ahead please."

Coach Banks was no longer looking at Jocko, but, rather,

yelling into the tunnel, calling back the team.

"Mr. Tognazzi, to speed things up here, we can all see you were petitioning the Commodore coaching staff to stop the music, but, at this point, what is Coach Banks saying? Just what is he doing here?"

"He's yelling at his team to come back. He was saying, you know, like, 'come back here you pussies and take care of business'... stuff like that." A low volume clamor began to hum behind in the crowd. "He wanted everyone back on the sideline."

"You realize, Mr. Tognazzi, if you remained on your side of the field, this wouldn't have erupted into the big fight that it did, right?"

"My side of the field?" complained Jocko. "The game was over and done. This was my field. This was Highlander turf. All of it. They could have all been in the showers already, man. But they had to kick the sleeping dog, turn the knife, all that kinda stuff. They had the right to play the football game; they didn't have the right to 'dis our field, break our rules." Shouts and claps came out from the very back of the gym. Others joined in.

The Chairman tapped his gavel. "All right. All right... that's enough. Mr. Tognazzi, thank you, that will be all." The Chairman leaned back and talked to a member one panelist down. Jocko walked back to his seat in the very front row, with coaching staff and linemen.

"The Board of Inquiry calls Mr. Bodie Houge, Altamont High School." People began to talk and murmur.

"Shit-- here goes." Bodie muttered as he stood up. Chase patted his back. As Bodie stepped over the long row of students and strangers, he glanced toward the back of the gym. It was packed. Standing room only. "Hoo boy... "

Standing on the far left hand side was Chrissy, with her arms folded. She must have gotten there at the last minute. She looked concerned.

"Mr. Houge, you are a team captain and starting quarterback for the Altamont High Highlander football team, are you not?"

"Yes sir, I am."

There was a brief pause. "Mr. Houge, could you come around the podium and have us have a look at you?"

Bodie snaked his way around the podium and a table that had microphone wires and boxes. The board looked at him more closely, some cringed slightly.

"What happened to your eye, Mr. Hogue?

"I was hit. I was hit with a..." Bodie stopped for a second. He did not want to say the word 'trombone.' "A horn of some kind. A brass... horn. The flared open end hit my eye socket."

"Okay. You can go back to the podium."

The Jumbo Tron began playing fight scenes at random. Some from Channel 8, some from cell phones. Some were taken from high in the bleachers, showing fighting going on all over the field and the sidelines. Other people were running all over the field.

"Mr. Houge, people all over California, including the Governor have called and asked me, 'what happened there?' Can I just ask you the same thing? You look like were in the middle of it all. Just what happened?"

"It's just one of those things where you just had to have been there," began Bodie. He was feeling better. Just being up there broke the ice. And he could tell they didn't chew out Jocko, who was guilty as hell. 'Tell them a nice story, Bodie and sit down,' he thought to himself.

"As you know, our school paper wrote an article on the anniversary of the big fight when Charter Stockton played at our school. We had voted not to play 'Gimme Shelter' the first time all those years ago, and Charter Stockton played it instead of our band and it was a big, big fight. So I guess the article woke up people's memories and, for some reason, their band played it again... for old time's sake, I guess."

The video stopped, the lights came on again. "Mr. Houge, were you aware that the Friday morning Stockton Record also wrote an article about the melee anniversary?"

Bodie was surprised. He didn't realize they ran a story too. He could only shake his head. "Mr. Chairman, I took a sociology class this quarter. It talked about..., uh..., 'group think.' Sometimes people think as a group in different terms as they would as an individual. I think it's why sometimes people get swept away in a big event, because they are only half-thinking for themselves but also with the big group, you know? Half mind reading, half spur-of-the-moment. Some people might call it a 'herd mentality', I was surprised hardly anyone knew about the anniversary. I didn't even know about the old fight until the bonfire almost a month ago. I guess it was already in a lot of people's heads as a... latent memory... just sitting there in the subconscious. I guess when their band played 'Gimmie Shelter' it was like... throwing gasoline on a smoldering fire. It was already there... and it just... blew up."

"I'm impressed Mr. Houge. You must have gotten an 'A' in your sociology class."

It took all that Bodie could do to suppress a laugh. "No sir. I'm not expecting any 'A'." There was mild laughter. Bodie was almost enjoying this now.

"Truth is Mr. Houge, this isn't the first time you went across the field to speak your mind, is it?

'Say what?' Bodie thought to himself. "I don't think I ever went over before, Mr. Chairman."

"Mr. Audio/Visual could you play clip 49, please?"

Bodie looked to the left. Some of the Freshmen and Sophomores that made up the Audio Visual club were operating the video with a couple of laptops. 'Oh crap.' Bodie Thought to himself. *'What shit do they have on me? Is this their way to get back at the seniors that gave them grief for stumbling onto the senior pits? Dang it. Didn't I stick up for their bony little asses?'*

Bodie could feel his heart beating in his throat. His jugular was going to burst. It really was. The lights dimmed again and the video began.

'Just take it like a man, Bodie. Face the music.'

The video was of a better quality. It was from the video camera that was mounted to a tripod up in the press box. The game 'film' was taken from this camera. It showed Bodie and the team singing the school song, just before the melee.

'Mommie.'

Then, while singing, Bodie looked at Chase and they began to walk away.

'Wait a minute. This wasn't last night's game...'

As they walked across the field, everyone could see this was the end of the Max Kolbe game. Strangely, thought Bodie, the camera zoomed out, then followed Bodie and Chase as they walked over to the Crusader circle as they sang their school song. The camera then began to slowly zoom in. You could clearly see Bodie put his arm on one of the big players and then that player put his hand on Bodie's shoulder pad. It then slowly zoomed out as other Highlanders came over and sang or hummed the Crusader school song.

"Umm, Bodie, why'd you do that? I mean why did you go over there? It was a close game, too, from what I've heard. Pretty hard fought game, right?"

"Yes. I just felt sorry for them. They lost it with no time left on the clock. It probably will keep them out of CIF. I just felt for them."

"Who is that? That you're talking to there?"

"Dominic Kanare. He'll be a starter in his Freshman year. At any FBS school."

"Good player?"

"Yeah."

"Knocked you down once or twice?"

"Bruised my ribs. Probably cracked Harrison's, our back-up QB."

"So... no trash talk, no punching... just hard-hitt'n football, huh?"

"Yeah. He was cool. He helped me up a few times. Good guy."

"So Mr. Kanare knocks you down, bruises your ribs, and you go over and say 'good game.'"

"Yes sir."

"Thank you, Mr. Houge. I don't think we have any more questions, do we gentlemen?" Bodie nodded, turned and began to walk back to his seat. As he turned a million flash bars went off. Channel 8 had a light source and a mini cam zoomed in his face. Quickly the light turned off and the cameraman poked his head out from behind his equipment. It was one of the oldsters from the bonfire. He smiled and waved. Bodie mouthed 'hey!' as he walked past.

"Not so bad, not so bad, my man." Chase shook Bodie's hand down low.

"What is going on? They're treating us like we're victims."

"I know it!" said Chase in a cheerfully upbeat voice. "Where did all that 'Soc come from, anyway? Dude! You sounded like Hagan up there! Geeze!"

"The board calls Coach Crutchfield to the podium please. Coach Crutchfield from Charter Stockton."

A crusty, stocky man in his late fifties, coach Crutchfield marched up dressed in his game shorts and a windbreaker over a Beefy Tee. You could tell where his cap had been, stamping his thick graying hair.

"Mr. Crutchfield, this is the second time this year that you've appeared before this board, is it not?"

"Yes, it is." said Crutchfield, his voice strong, almost defiant.

"The fact is in mid August we were addressing some

concerns from out of league coaching staffs that your team had displayed acts of taunting on a consistent basis during last season. We decided if there was any more evidence of taunting from your program, we would issue sanctions appropriately. But, to your credit Coach Crutchfield, your team, for the most part, had been playing in a very sportsman-like manner... all season. That is, until the Altamont game. I don't know if it was pent up or something, but then... a volcano of ill will and hooliganism. What happened?"

"Everything was fine, sir, until after the game. Heck, we were going into the tunnel. It was a done deal. Next thing we know, there's Altamont players all up and down our sideline. In our face, in our band's face, just look'n for a fight. They just plain started it, sir. Just plain and simple."

Without making eye contact, the Chairman shuffled some papers and continued. "Mr. Crutchfield, it has come to our attention that two linemen and a linebacker now playing on your team didn't start last year. Mr. Jackson, Mr. Johnson and Mr. Terry. These great starters didn't start last year. Why is that?"

"They moved into our district early last summer. We were glad to let them tryout for our team. They were obviously talented and they each earned a spot on our starting roster."

"Uh huh," said the Chairman, still not making eye contact. "Coach, it was brought to our attention a few weeks ago that these men are here without their families. Who are they living with?"

"Sir, these young men are staying with area families until their family situations are resolved."

"Oh. I see. They had a little strife at home so they re-located 400 miles away from their nearest relative to go to

Charter Stockton High School. Just who is that they are staying with, anyway?"

"Umm, families. Just families in the area..."

"The fact is they are staying with the Muleskinners, are they not?"

"Beg... beg your pardon?"

"They are not with families, are they? They are with single men, all members of a psuedo booster club for athletics. A club called the Muleskinners, am I right?"

"To my knowledge, maybe one or two are..."

"You realize this is in direct violation to our out-of-district bylaws, are you not?"

"I haven't looked into it, sir."

"Another thing I am having a hard time figuring out is your band, just whipping up the tune 'Gimmie Shelter.' They seemed to, just, all of sudden, start playing it from memory. It just doesn't seem practical."

"I wouldn't know about such things, Mr. Chairman."

"No, I wouldn't expect that you would, being the football coach and all. Stay where you are Mr. Crutchfield. The Board would like to call Mr. Choate, the band director to the front, please. Mr. Choate.

A younger man, in his early thirties, came walking up briskly from the very back. He had a thick mane of brown hair, a slender nose and breathed through his mouth. He dressed nicely in a sport coat and an oxford shirt.

"Mr. Choate, I'd like to have you share the microphone at

the podium, if you could, with Coach Crutchfield. Mr. Choate, when you do a muscial program, a halftime show, or a parade... you have to practice your music, am I right?"

"Yes sir, that you do. Over and over."

"So if you have a game on Friday night, your band starts practicing a week or so ahead of time, or thereabouts, right?"

"Usually, yes. I have music run off the week previously, and then we have band practice the whole week prior to the game."

"So on Monday afternoon you were practicing 'Gimmie Shelter.'"

Mr. Choate paused. "Er, no, sir. Not that Monday."

"Well, then, just what did you practice Monday?"

"Those Magnificent Men and Their Flying Machines." Mr. Choate made a nervous glance at Coach Crutchfield.

"What made you change your mind, Mr. Choate?"

"There were requests for 'Gimmie Shelter' and so I changed it. I am relatively new here and didn't know the history behind the selection, so I went ahead and switched the songs. It seemed harmless at the time, really."

"Who requested the change, Mr. Choate?" The Chairman was again looking at printed sheets of notes and the syllabus.

"I did, Mr. Chairman," injected Coach Crutchfield.

"Why did you do a thing like that, Coach?"

"With so much water under the bridge, I thought it was just a memory of a time gone by. A 'remember when' moment.

A 'hey, I remember that', or 'where was I when that happened' event."

A note was handed to the far left board member. He read it and passed it on, which was relayed to the next member, on to the Chairman.

"Commissioner..., Mr. Chairman, it was nostalgia. Nothing more," pleaded Coach Crutchfield.

The chairman read the note as the coach made his case. "Mr. Crutchfield, where did you play your high school ball?"

"What?"

"You heard me. Where did you play high school football?"

"Charter Stockton."

"Were you at that game all those years ago? At the first melee?"

Coach Crutchfield didn't answer. He he just stood there steaming, but biting his lip. He hadn't lost his job yet. He didn't want to blow it. But he was pissed. He was being played.

"Coach Crutchfield: were you at that game? Just tell us."

"I was there. I didn't do anything to be ashamed of. I was just there." He didn't wait to be dismissed. He just pulled his cap out of the small of his back and fastened it to his head as he turned and marched down the aisle and exited the gym, with a million eyeballs drilling into his back.

"Whoa. What just happened, man?" wondered Bodie aloud.

CJ finally spoke up. "I think Crutchfield is going to keep

walking until he gets to, like, Texas, because there's nothing here to keep him around."

The Chairman thanked Mr. Choate and released him.

"This Board of Inquiry has asked all of its questions. We will render our report on Tuesday afternoon. This meeting is adjourned." With that he pounded the gavel one last time. It was drowned out by the gaggle of over a thousand parents, students and teachers. Chrissy came up and gave Bodie a big hug.

"I'll wait for you at my house, okay?"

"Okay." Bodie was seemingly being washed away by the throng of people trying to get to the exit. Seeing the media looking at him and Chase, they began to fight their way to the nearest door.

9
SATURDAY NIGHT'S ALL RIGHT

"LISTEN, BOYS: I'M ASKING YOU, PLEASE; no drinking tonight. No fighting. I know you want to celebrate, but after all you've been through I know some of you are going to over-do-it." Mr. Houge was doing that weird parental thing where they can issue an order, but all the while sound like they're pleading for common sense. "I know these things." He was driving them home, but lecturing through the rear-view mirror.

"Yes, Mr. Houge." They all replied in a foot dragging fashion.

"You know. Movie and a pizza. Good clean fun."

Chase, always the professional, agreed. "That's fine with me, Mr. Houge. I've got one foot out of high school as it is, and I don't want to mess up my scholarship. But you know what? I think Bodie is more worried for my scholarship than I am."

"Well, he should be. I hope you all look out for each other. All of you."

"I'm fine with movie and a pizza," added Chase. "Melissa is working tonight. I can see her after the movie in the food court."

CJ rolled his eyes. "Then I'm going for the real stuff; Holy Grail Pizza. None of that pizza-on-a-stick factory-made stuff. I'll be in the pizza parlor."

"I'm sure you can all work something out. Listen, pizza's on me tonight, okay? I mean it. Just no drink'n, okay?" Mr. Houge was going to seal this deal. They all readily agreed. He dropped them all off at their homes. CJ wanted to take a nap and Chase wanted to watch college football. Bodie just wanted to lay down with an ice pad. Unless some bird of grade forgiveness flew into the administration's window, he was going to sit out the remainder of this season. But, deep down, something told him he might still have a chance.

"I think it's great your dad is springing for pizza for all of us. That's really great." Chrissy finally got to have Bodie to herself, albeit for only the drive over to the mall. Then she would have to share him with C.J. and Chase, but that was fine.

"Finals are done, the biggest game of the season is behind me... I feel free somehow," said Bodie. "I'm done with trying to control things I don't really control."

"Well, you can control your grades, you know..."

"Yeah, but I waited until the last minute. I screwed myself. I painted myself into a corner, as it were. I gave myself all the rope I needed to hang myself. I ran with scissors and took wooden nickels. I considered burning a bridge..."

"Shut up, shut up, shut up." Chrissy gave Bodie a big french kiss while he tried to keep his eyes on the road.

As they came up for air, a glassy eyed Bodie realized something. "And best of all: I don't have to read another chapter of Hunchback of Notre Dame! Chrissy burrowed her head into his shoulder. They motored on to the Mall to meet the others. The sun had already set behind the Altamont, the red lights on the giant windmills were on to ward off lost airplanes, and the Altamont Renaissance Fashion Mall stood in front of them, almost a silhouette. The parking lot lights and other lighting had not come on yet.

"Oooo spooky." Teased Chrissy.

"Let me out, okay?" said Bodie with a pang of pain. He was sitting at one of the only booths in the food court of the Mall, sandwiched between Hector and Jocko on one side and Chrissy and Chase on the other. They were still talking about "Burnt Fort," the movie they had just seen at the Oh Max! theatre.

"Was there ever any fort overtaken by the Indians?" wondered Hector.

"Probably not," said Jocko in a dismissive tone. "I think the whole plot was just Hollywood's attempt to make the 'Injun bite the dust, just one more time."

"'Scuse'm. Me pissum' bad." Bodie resorted to some really bad humor to get out of the tight booth. "Why don't some of you sit with CJ? It's too crowded here." CJ had brought back a small pizza from Holy Grail Pizza. He wanted to sit with his friends, and the Holy Grail didn't really like minors in their place after ten PM. Gena was talking to Chase and Melissa at the counter of Bad Dog. Melissa wasn't getting off until midnight. But at this hour business was slow, except for a few impulse buys' by passer-bys from the late movies letting out.

The last movie had let out. It was now past eleven p.m.

and most of the mall shops were closed. The individual fashion shops had their roll-up barriers locked down. There was no Musak playing, making the mall echo with each footfall and conversation. The large anchor stores were also locked shut. All that was left were stragglers walking the gauntlet from the theatres to the main west exit via the food court. Bodie gravitated to the bathrooms halfway to the theatres. There was a woman's bathroom in the food court, but not a men's, for some reason. There was one inside of Holy Grail Pizza, but if you weren't a patron and under 21, they would always give you a dirty look. Not really thinking of anything in particular, Bodie stared at the free-standing medieval clock down at the center of the Mall. He would usually meet friends there. He suddenly remembered that Chrissy was going to tell him something there earlier in the week, but he had to break off the date. What was it? Why hadn't she told him since? Something about Chase?

A man in his thirties walked out of the men's room and began a big kissing play with his wife or girlfriend. Bodie didn't like walking around the older crowd while they made out. Weren't they past all that? They were suddenly aware that they were not alone and they abruptly disengaged.

"Hi Mrs. Horner." Bodie said, out of rote, trying to remember his manners before realizing she wasn't kissing Mr. Horner, the Dean. "Mr. Parks. How are you..." Bodie and Mr. Parks watched each other's pupils dilate.

Bodie's memory rapid fired about how Dean Horner was so grouchy and that Melissa had said his marriage was on the rocks. "Hi Bodie. Have a good weekend." With that, Mr. Parks and Mrs. Horner turned as one and walked away, leaning into the air before them. As Bodie relieved himself at the urinal, he wondered if his typing grade would improve any. His concentration was disturbed by another theatre patron using the urinal next to his. He was in his late twenties, with matted blonde hair and a heavy jacket. He smelled of campfire. Bodie washed his hands and left.

"Did the faculty hand in their grades yet?" Bodie wondered as he approached the food court booth. Gena was just walking back to the tables to join Jocko and CJ. Hector and Chrissy were still in the booth. Chase was kissing Melissa over the counter. "What has gotten into those two?" thought Bodie. "Two weeks ago they were thrown together as king and queen of Homecoming. And now they were in love."

"Everyone is in love, like it's springtime or something," said Bodie as he began to lower himself back into the booth. Just as his butt touched the bench, he felt a 'zzzzzzzzzt' whiz past his head.

'Bam!' A shot rang out. Then another. Hector flew backwards in the booth. Instinctively, Bodie pushed Chrissy down below the tabletop. 'Bam!' People began screaming. The gunshots made an immediate echo off the ceiling and walls. Someone was walking from the west entrance, which now was the only exit from the Mall, and firing two hand guns at the nearest living targets. Bodie heard one round ricochet off the top of the table. He and Chrissy looked at Hector clinch his bloodied chest. Then, Hector suddenly relaxed. *"Is he dead?"* Bodie wondered. To his right he saw Gena lying down, eyes open wide.

"Let's get the hell outta here!" Bodie growled through clenched teeth. Chrissy grabbed her backpack as they scrambled from underneath the table. "Bam! Bam!" More shots, but this time not directed at them. As Chase yelled at Melissa to run out the back of Bad Dog, two rounds hit him in the back. He was trying to shield her as he yelled. His body slowly slid off the counter top onto the floor.

By this time Bodie and Chrissy ran after Jocko and CJ and a dozen other food court patrons already in full flight away from the shooter. Bodie sneaked a peek at the shooter. He methodically marched toward the Holy Grail Pizza Pub. He wore a ski mask and a dark jacket with jeans and hiking boots. Some of the patrons inside had come to the entrance to see exactly what was going on, but the employees were already headed for the back kitchen and exit. About eight people were caught in a dead end of booths inside the Pub section. Bodie kept running toward the Oh Max theatres. As they ran, they could hear screams and rapid fire gunshots from the Holy Grail Pizza Pub.

As they neared the Oh Max, Jocko could see a girl inside locking the glass doors. Probably not because of the gunfire, but that it was simply closing time. "Hey! Open up! Open up!" He bellowed. She was dimly aware something was amiss, but left the doors locked anyway and tried to wave them off. But as more and more people cleared the planters in the mall, running at full pace, she froze trying to comprehend the emergency. But before they could reach the Oh Max, a man emerged from the bathroom Bodie had just used minutes before, wearing a green ski mask with an ecology logo sewn atop it. He wore a heavy jacket.

"I know him. He was pissin' when I left the bathroom..." Bodie said as he screeched to a halt, holding Chrissy's wrist. Everyone was in front of them as the gunman pulled out two pistols from his jacket. He began shooting, rapid fire; a little wild at first, but people began grabbing their chests and stomachs, trying to scurry off in a bent over fashion. Some not so much running, but falling without falling down.

There was no chance of making it to the Oh Max, even if the doors were opened by the scared employee. Bodie looked back again and saw that the other masked man was now back out in the mall and marching towards them, changing clips in his guns as he approached. The people in front of them who were still ambulatory were running for the cover of about four or five planters. They were landscaped with evergreen shrubs and artificial palm trees. They were in the area of the Italian stonework and faux windows. The Medieval clock loomed above them in the middle of one of the larger planters. How many times Bodie had looked at this clock, with its stars and moon phases. One hand even had the sun on the end to show the seasons. There were the figurines of everyday people of Renaissance Italy. Eerily, along with the people was a skeleton. Maybe it was there to remind people that time is running out; better not waste it. But in this horrible moment, Bodie felt like he was the grim reaper, looking down to make a morbid body count.

Bodie didn't want to follow the crowd into the dead end of the proposed addition. It would be their death. But there was no where else to go except toward a shooter. In the backfield of football his instincts always came up with a quick solution. But not now. Chrissy took over, pulled him by the wrist to the nearest door. Bodie didn't like it, the door was exposed.

"Chrissy-- no. These doors don't have a doorknob. No push bar. They're one-way..." Bodie was shielded by a palmtree from the faraway shooter, who was busy shooting at the closest targets. But the one with the ecology symbol was bearing in straight at them, taking aim with both guns.

"Please...!" Chrissy cried as she banged on the sealed door out of wreckless desperation.

"We gotta go. We gotta go now!" Bodie was staring at the masked gunman. He was only 25 feet away. He was trying to shoot people with both hands; trying to target and fire. Maybe it was more of a detriment than an advantage for killing the most people in the shortest amount of time.

"Please..." Chrissy sobbed. Bodie began to shield Chrissy. She had her book bag with her still. A bullet hit the Italian stonework next to Bodie's head. Maybe running to the planters was their only option. Then, suddenly, the door cracked open. They could see one eye looking at them, hesitating. Then it swung open about two feet. "Get in!" a voice inside ordered. Bodie and Chrissy ran in, stooped in a hunch, ducking bullets. The door slammed shut behind them.

Mr. Hagan loosened his tie and fell into his easy chair. He turned on the Channel 8 Late Night News. It was already on, reporting on a car crash high up on the Altamont. Then a live feed clumsily cut in. "This is Heidi Cutler live at the Altamont Renaissance Fashion Mall. We are getting first hand reports of a shooting inside the Mall and it is still ongoing from our latest interviews. A few mall employees escaped out of their private entrances and all say there is a shooter firing at people at random. The San Joaquin County Sheriff's SWAT team is gearing up to assault the interior of the mall. So far only one victim has been removed from inside and is being rushed to Altamont General--."

"Oh no. Not another shooting," sighed Mr. Hagan. "Not here."

"Thud-- thud!" The three of them turned and looked at two indentations made by bullets that impacted the steel door.

Bodie stared incredulously at the man who had saved them. He had a black jacket, a beanie over jet black hair. He was pale but not thin. His eyes were dark as well. A very deep, dark brown. It was the Mall Dweller.

"How'd you get to us? How..."

"No time. Come on. Follow me. There's a security office down the corridor. Maybe we can save your friends."

Obediently they followed the Mall Dweller until they came to an intersection. Up a flight of stairs was a group of office windows and lots of light.

"Oh-nine oh-nine. Oh nine... you out there? Oh nine." A scratchy voice kept calling. It was muffled inside of his jacket. The Mall Dweller paused and pulled out a really small walkie talkie of sorts. It wasn't a Nextel phone, it was something high tech. Bodie hadn't noticed it before, but the Mall Dweller had ear buds. He pulled them out and answered his radio.

"Oh nine at the base. Comin' up with survivors. Has PD shown up yet?

"No: they are alerting county sheriff SWAT team; nothing yet."

"Any sign of Marky and Jeff?"

"No. I'm scanning all angles. I'm finding bodies..."

Bodie followed the Mall Dweller up the exterior stairs to the security office. He realized the Mall Dweller worked here. As they walked in Bodie and Chrissy could see a long counter and multiple flat screens monitoring the entire mall. Some had screen within screen views. "If you look just outside of the Oh Max doors, you'll find them," said Bodie. "I think they were the first ones shot by the ecology shooter."

The Security guard behind the counter pushed a button and used the joystick to look over the entrance to the theatres. He zoomed in on a few bodies near the ticket office. Sure enough, two men in white long sleeve shirts lying on the ground face down. They were all quiet for just a second. The security guard had thin black glasses, which he moved down his nose and rubbed his eyes. The Mall Dweller, regaining his composure looked up. "Zoom in on axis addition."

Dutifully the security guard zoomed in on the area with the planters. The gunmen had over a dozen people huddled behind brick planters. The plywood barrier to the addition was behind them. "They're still shooting, but not moving any closer. I don't get it," said the Mall Dweller.

Bodie studied the scene. He saw Jocko pop up in a certain stance... then CJ doing the same thing; at the same time they came out of their little 'windup' and threw something. "They're throwing rocks at them. From the planters..." Bodie said, upbeat.

"That could buy them some time." the Mall Dweller said.

Bodie was happy. He looked at Chrissy. She looked tired, almost sleepy.

"What's the matter? Chrissy?" She was rubbing her back.

"I'm all wet back here..." She pulled her hand out from between the backpack and her back. It was dark red; all bloodied.

"Chrissy!"

She fainted at the sight of her own blood. The Mall Dweller helped to put her down gently.

"She musta got shot as we closed the door. I think the back pack saved her. The angle... she must have got a shot from the other shooter..., either he missed and a stray shot got her as you jumped in the door. I think he was using hollow tipped bullets..., see how it mushroomed out? Or, he was aiming from his end of the planters and just got lucky."

"The ambulances are pulling up outside." said the security guard. "No sign of SWAT. Here comes some PD..."

"Okay. Let's get her to the ambulance ASAP." Outside of the security office was a parking garage structure with its own staircase. The street between the two structures became an assembly point for the ambulances and, now, police. Bodie talked to the emergency medical techs as they loaded Chrissy into the ambulance. The Mall Dweller talked to the police sergeant.

"Chrissy, you want me to come?"

"No... get CJ and Jocko. Help them." With that she began to cry. An EMT shoved her gurney into the back and slammed the door. They were gone in seconds. More ambulances drove up, lights blazing.

The Mall Dweller stomped over to Bodie. "They're going to wait for the SWAT." The Mall Dweller motioned his thumb at the lone police car. "By that time your buddies will all be dead-- can you help?"

"Yeah. Whatever it takes."

"Come on." They ran back up the stairwell to the Security Offices. The police sergeant followed suit. "I'm going in to take these guys down. I need you to be an extra set of eyes. Will you do that for me?

"Yeah. Yeah." Bodie kept pace with the Mall Dweller as he took big strides back up the office.

"Don't need you to take any risks. Just look around. Look for the second shooter. Look for a possible third shooter. Just look behind me, to my sides, okay?"

"Yeah. 'Got it."

"If there is a shooter, just say 'Tahiti.' Tahiti six o'clock. Behind me. My 'six.' Or Tahiti nine o'clock, my left side... you know like a clock... like the WWII pilots."

"Yeah... I got it. I got it." Bodie was following the Mall Dweller back into the Security Office.

"Graham; this is Sergeant Lambert. He's going to be liaison officer to the SWAT team. They're inbound. ETA eight or nine minutes. Also, I want you to keep in touch with Danny in the Summit Ambulance. He'll come in when others won't. Okay?"

"Gotcha, Chief."

The Mall Dweller left Sergeant Lambert behind. The police officer already made his case for no one to go back into the mall. At a locker, the Mall Dweller pulled out a key ring with about thirty keys on it. He opened a locker, even though it had a combination lock on it. He put the key into a key hole in the middle of the tumbler. The locker opened, and the Mall Dweller took out a dangerous looking rifle. He dredged hand fulls of ammo and poured them into his jacket pockets. He looked at Bodie as he loaded up.

"What's your name?"

"Bodie. Bodie Houge. Yours?"

"Just call me Jake. I'm a private police officer. Undercover for now. I carry guns, arrest people and shoot them if necessary."

"I think it is necessary right now, man."

"Yeah. I know. They're your friends. If we can get in right now, we might save them. Kooks like these usually shoot themselves when confronted by someone with a gun. This is a

Mini 14. It's a compact version of the M14. A lot of Vietnam soldiers didn't want the M16 when they were in a firefight. They would keep the M-14 throughout the war. Shooting at these guys with a rifle may be enough. It might be just that easy. Columbine taught us you have to go in. Right away. I'm not so sure about San Joaquin's finest. I think they're out there right now wringing their hands. That won't work."

Jake looked up at the monitor. CJ must have of scored a hit on the terrorist with the black hood. He was blotting blood coming out of his mouth. A rock must have hit teeth and tissue. Bodie was so proud of CJ, scoring that hit.

"Let's go. They're just getting them mad at this point."

"Some kind of hippie van just pulled up at the West entrance," said Graham. "'Might be an extraction team...'"

"If that's the case we don't have much time. They're going to kill as many people as they can and leave. They aren't on a suicide mission," said Jake, now worried.

Bodie followed Jake the Mall Dweller down a corridor. He could tell Jake was still figuring out what to do, how to approach the terrorists. "I think these guys are Hetch 22. They gotta be."

In a corridor they could hear crying. Faint at first, it was definite now, coming closer, just around the corner. It was a girl sobbing. Bodie went ahead, sticking his head around the corner.

"Melissa!" shouted Bodie. "Are you okay?" Melissa had blood over her Bad Dog blouse. Bodie lifted it and didn't see any wounds. He was amazed at the size of her breasts. He felt guilty for gawking. "Chase covered me as I ran from the counter. They must of killed him. I just ran with some of the others. I lost them. I think they found a way to the parking lot. I knew where the security office was. I thought I could warn them. I thought..." Her voice trailed off into a series of sobs.

"It's okay. Keep going. The police are up there. They'll take care of you. We're going to save CJ and Jocko... all of the others stuck in there. We gotta go. Okay?" Melissa knodded and walked on slowly, her arms cradling her stomach. She only looked down.

Jake was already making his way down the corridor that led to Bodie and Chrissy's rescue. "Were you in the military?" asked Bodie.

"Yeah. Three years. Military Police. Afterward I joined a private Police Agency. I did some performance driving for the security of celebrities. I was slated to go over to the Pacific Rim and do bodyguard work for a Sultan. They assigned me to Altamont while I waited for my assignment. Now this."

Halfway down to the door, Jake stopped, and looked at a service door. He fumbled with some keys and finally opened it. They could hear more shots beginning just outside, followed by screams.

Quasimoto assisted them, having no suspicion-- poor deaf creature!-- of their fatal intentions; it was the vagabond crew whom he regarded as the enemies of the Egyptian. He himself conducted Tristan the Hermit to every possible place of concealment, opened for him all the secret doors, the double bottomed altars, and the back sacristies. Hunchback of Notre Dame

"If we go out the same door they might bushwack us," stated Jake. "Maybe this way we can bushwack them." Jake pulled out and fully opened the short utility service door. They stooped down and entered the service door that was only four feet high and had a vent. There were no lights in the low, narrow chute. Electrical conduit and fuse boxes lined the service way. At the end was another small utility door. Through its vent they could see the shooter with the black hood holding only one gun and dabbing his mouth with the free hand. They were now closing in on the remaining victims. Bodie was amazed; they were inside the medieval clock he had stared at for so many years. He now saw that it was just a bunch of servos and electric motors; no gears or movements.

Jake motioned to Bodie to quietly open the utility door. Bodie made room for Jake to move out. There was some creaking in the henges and friction on the floor of the planter that they were in, but the gunfire drowned it out. Jake leaned out and rose with the gunsight already to his eye. He fired two quick shots-- a double tap. The terrorist didn't know what hit him. He was too busy shooting at CJ and Jocko. Bodie took a quick scan for any other shooters. Immediately he saw the ecology shooter, with both guns trained on them. He was only twenty feet away, behind the clock mount.

"Tahiti! Seven o'clock!" barked Bodie.

Like a cat, Jake swiftly rotated around with the gunsight still glued to his eye. He began to fire at the exact time as the eco terrorist. In a half-hunch, Bodie saw the terrorist go down. Bodie saw a spray of pink between himself and Jake. He worried Jake may have been hit, but before he could ask, Bodie found himself looking at the ceiling: the skylights were black. There was a commotion of women crying and shouting, their cries bouncing off the mall interiors. The Italian stonework absorbed only a little of the confused sounds of relieved patrons and gunshot victims. As Bodie stared at the black skylight, he could see a jetliner fly over with its navigation lights on, during its decent into the Bay Area. The plane and the skylight were eclipsed by CJ's fat head and further more by Jocko's.

"You okay man? You shot? You're shot, dude!" They lifted him onto some green leafy plants.

"Did he get him? Did Jake kill 'em?" asked Bodie, now groggy.

"Yeah! You guys saved our sorry asses!" cried CJ.

"Yeah, you guys came outta nowhere," recounted Jocko. "That's him; that's the Mall Dweller, isn't it?" Jocko took off his belt and made a tourniquet for Bodie's arm.

"Where am I hit?"

"You got it in the bicep." Jocko halted when he realized the injury.

"Bodie baby... it's your throwin' arm, man. Geeze I'm sorry. I'm really sorry!" CJ sounded as if he had shot Bodie.

Jake ran up shouting into his hi-tech walkie talkie. "Just tell Danny to come in through the car display door windows... he'll know what I'm talking about. The others will follow him— hold on a sec."

Jake stared at Bodie, realizing he had been hit. "Bodie, I'm sorry man. It was a lucky hit. I am really sorry." He paused a moment. "I gotta open the doors for the ambulances. They can drive right in and help you and everyone who got hit." With that, he ran to some windows near the Oh Max and sorted through his key ring. Within moments, he was pushing a series of large windows that rolled on hidden tracks until four large widows stacked in front of each other. The first ambulance came in while its tires lightly squeaked on the polished mall floors. The first one stopped where Jake squatted after rolling the windows open. He was double checking his fellow security guards, finding them lifeless. Another ambulance barreled in, followed by two more. The SWAT team ran in alongside the remaining ambulances.

Danny got out of the first ambulance and decided to forgo any triage; they would just load up the living injured and just lay tarps on the deceased. The ER could perform the triage over the radio and be ready by the time the ambulance arrived at the door.

Jake and CJ brought Bodie over from the planter. Danny and his blonde co-driver eased Bodie into the gurney. The Channel 8 news van drove into the mall, its driver wearing a 'why not?' expression on his face. Heidi Cutler bailed out of the van and aimed her microphone vaguely at the action, hoping someone would answer her blunt questions.

Jake stared at Bodie and then talked to him in a low voice. "I think the ecology shooter was Commander Plastique. It sure looks like him. We got 'em, man. I looked at his bullets: they were full metal jacket, not hollow tips. Your wound may not be so traumatic, believe it or not..."

"Hey: that's the Altamont quarterback..., you know, from the hearings!" said the camera man, a man in his late-forties with metal rimmed glasses. "I talked to him at the bonfire... I think his name is Buddy."

"Buddy? Are you sure?"

"No. Something like that."

"Buddy: what is your name? Is it Buddy?"

Bodie tried to focus on the new arrivals. More news vans rolled in, the lights on their cameras lit up and were aimed right him. "What's your name? Who shot you?"

"What is his name?" The late arrivals asked Heidi.

"I don't know. He's the quarterback at Altamont." The EMTs loaded Bodie and his gurney onto the back of the ambulance. For a moment they stood him up until room could be made inside.

"What's your name!"

"My name is..." Bodie's voice trailed off, his eyes wandered, spying the skylights above the Italian stonework and the clock.

"Back off, he's slipping into shock-- ready?" The blonde EMT shouted to Danny. She climbed in, about to feed the gurney to Danny.

"Your name! What's your name?" Screached Heidi.

"My name... my name is..." Bodie looked at the skeleton again. The skeleton was still smiling at him and telling him to have a nice ride. High above the clock a mysterious silhouette clambered about the balustrade.

"My name is... Quasimotooo!" Jake slammed the door shut, hit the window twice with his open palm. The ambulance sped away on the polished floor to the exit.

The SWAT captain began to yell at Jake about procedure and the danger of another shooter lurking about. They exchanged tantrums. Jake said he wanted less chalk lines and more survivors. He thought the results would bear him out. The camera crews were escorted away to a safe distance while more survivors were stabilized and loaded up for the trip to Altamont General Hospital.

"You don't have to wait up for him, dad. He'll come in on his own. So what if he said he'd be in by midnight? He's out with his friends. He'll stay out as long as he wants. He's such an asshole that way sometimes," bitched Katy. Her father ignored her, surfing the TV channels over his crumpled newspaper.

"This is Heidi Cutler inside the Altamont Renaissance Fashion Mall. The shooters inside the Mall have been shot and the victims are being whisked away to Altamont General Hospital. The SWAT team is still trying to secure the area. Earlier, a few moments ago, an escape vehicle, a van, was shot repeatedly by SWAT officers for not stopping and possibly trying to run over the members of the SWAT team. We're still awaiting word on any survivors inside the van."

Mr. Houge read the byline at the bottom of the TV screen. 'Altamont Mall Shooting.' Stunned, he turned to the Sacramento stations. They were all reporting on it. Mr. Houge dropped his remote and sat in his recliner, slightly slouched. Katy stared at the screen and began to slowly cry.

10
POST-MORTEM

BODIE COULD HEAR AN AMBULANCE FAR AWAY. It never got closer but it wasn't left behind, either. Was it following him?

"Buddy! Buddy!" There was a pretty blonde lady looking over him. She had a staight nose and straight-cut bangs underneath a navy blue baseball cap. The cap read 'Summit.' She had a matching navy blue jacket. "Buddy! I need you to wake up. Stay awake. I want you to cough for me. Hear me? Cough!"

None of this was making any sense to Bodie. The faraway ambulance just wouldn't go away or catch up. 'Who's Buddy, anyway?' Bodie coughed.

"I need a real cough. Come on!" The Blonde lady rotated away, grabbing something from the ice chest on the floor. Bodie coughed two big coughs. Suddenly, the blonde EMT shoved an ice pack on the back of Bodie's neck.

"Aaah! What's that?" Then without any warning the EMT

unbuckled Bodie's belt and undid his jeans. She yanked down his underwear and shoved another ice pack underneath his scrotum.

"Dang! What the hell--?" The EMT didn't elaborate. She began working on another high schooler with a Max Kolbe letterman jacket across from him. Within moments she stood in a half crouch looking ahead.

"Danny: how much further?"

"Three minutes--- tops."

"'They ready for us?"

"Yeah. They're waiting."

Bodie was coming out of his stupor. The ambulance noise he heard was the one he was riding in. He watched the trees lining the street pass over him. Then the high rise hospital rose above him and slid past. It was eclipsed by the awning of the emergency entrance. They rushed the Max Kolbe kid out first.

"He's not responding. Get him into the trauma unit-- stat!" Bodie couldn't tell if a group of nurses, surgeons, or orderlies grabbed his gurney and ran off with him. The EMT turned back to him. The driver was shoving his gurney out and the blonde snapped the wheels down for the trip to the automatic doors. No one was left for Bodie. The EMTs rushed him into the ER. Bodie grimaced as he yanked the ice pack out of his pants and threw it at a hallway wall.

"Dang it, my balls are blue man." They ran over a door jamb. Bodie grimaced again. "My arm hurts. It's throbbing. Something's wrong..." The EMT looked irritated. She looked at an IV hanging above Bodie. It had plasma in it, but now it was nearly empty.

"Buddy, do you know your blood type?"

"Umm... 'O', I think."

"You sure?"

A surgeon looked Bodie over and talked to Danny. Two nurses came over from the Kolbe kid's table. They had been giving him CPR off and on in the ambulance, and now in the ER, but now they stopped. They were looking at the clock.

"All right, lets get started. They found his blood type in the system. 'O' negative." The doctor could see Bodie leaning up, asking the EMT a question. He got his team together and they began to stabilize Bodie's on again /off again shock.

As the EMT's began to grab their gurney to leave, the doctor asked, "What was he asking about?"

She hesitated. "He wanted to know if you were going to amputate."

Bodie came out of a slumber. He felt so good! He thought he must have slept for ten hours. He stretched. He even sported a woody.

"Ouch!" He had forgotten about his arm. His eyes looked at a smooth gray ceiling. He also forgot he was in the hospital. He had two IV's hooked up to him along with some wires to a monitor.

"Well. It's about time you woke up." A Philippino nurse was walking around with a tray, sliding the curtains away from the window. It was a sunny autumn afternoon.

"What time is it?" Asked Bodie, making sure his woody was covered up.

"It's One o'clock."

"Oh... I overslept."

"Tuesday. You have visitors. We have sent them up. Only two at a time. Your parents first. They very worried."

She floated out of the room. There was another bed by the window, but it was unoccupied. 'Tuesday?' Bodie wondered, in disbelief.

"Hey, hey, hey. How you doing, boy?" Bodie's dad was in his work shirt. *'Must have gotten off early today.'* Bodie thought. "I'm feeling good, feeling good. A little thirsty." As if on cue, the nurse walked in pushing a mobile tray with a water pitcher on it and a cup of ice. She poured him a cup, but as she left she gave a grave, serious look at the parents; some kind of warning. Bodie picked up on it, but he just didn't care. His mom gave him a big hug as his dad supervised. They avoided any and all bad news about people killed at the mall. But they assured Bodie that CJ and Jocko were fine and that they were going to drop in today.

Just as the conversation was getting boring someone in a wheelchair cruised in.

"Chrissy!"

"Hey look, it's Chrissy..." Bodie's dad noted the obvious.

"Only two guests at a time," teased Mrs. Houge.

"I was breakin' da law breakn' da law..." sang Chrissy, sort of, the Judas Priest song. They hugged and caught up, making sure they were going to recover, small stuff.

"How 'bout Melissa?" asked Bodie. "'She okay? She had blood on her, but I didn't see any wounds..."

"She didn't get hit," sighed Chrissy. "Chase shielded her till she made it out the back way."

"Bodie, they don't want you getting despondent over the victims..." Mr. Houge cautioned. "Maybe you shouldn't talk about them for a while. They have some crisis counselors that are going to talk to you and your friends a little later on..., okay?"

"Yeah, okay dad. I think I know who made it and who didn't. I just have to let it sink it a bit." Bodie stared at Chrissy, smiling. "Did Melissa get a boob job or something? I couldn't help but to notice..." Bodie's parents were astounded. "What!"

"Well, I saw, uh..."

"Bodie... I was going to tell you. By the clock that day, remember?"

"Yeah...?"

"But you canceled and then Melissa made me promise not to tell you..."

"'Bout a boob job."

"No! You dumb ass!" Chrissy looked at his parents, but they were puzzled, too.

"Melissa is pregnant. For a while. They were seeing each other since Hell Week."

"Whaaaau...?" Said Bodie, in a Scooby Do vernacular.

"She was funny about announcing their being 'steady.' She was always funny about stuff like that. She was accepted at Santa Clara, and he was in at Stanford, and it's, like, 30 minutes away from each other. So they were going to make it public at the homecoming. But they were an item long before that. He was at the Mall all the time, you big dummy." Bodie suddenly realized Chase's huge gaps of missing time, until the homecoming dance. Then they were seemingly an item.

"Dang. That 'ol dog." Bodie shook his head. His dad smiled, his mother made it clear she disapproved. But she realized Chase was dead and had a sad smile appear on her lips.

"Chase's parents know now. Melissa told them after Saturday night. They were ecstatic! It was like a part of Chase was still here, just around the corner."

They talked and laughed for a while. Bodie changed the subject.

"So, the shooters... Hetch 22, right?"

"They don't want us talking about all that," said Mr. Houge, putting a lid on it all. "But, just to let you know, yeah. It was Hetch 22. The SWAT team killed everyone in the van, outside of the mall. Hetch 22 also exploded a van on the dam itself at the same time the shooting was going on. It didn't even put a dent in the dam. Just bent a guard rail. They caught twelve of them at the border, just before Tijuana. They found a campsite up in the Sierras, but it looked abandoned for some time..."

"I think that was the lot of them," said Mrs. Houge with a dismissive snort. "I think after the murder rampage, they don't have any sympathy from environmental groups."

"Man."

A doctor walked briskly in, staring intermittently at a clipboard. "Hi everyone, I'm Dr. Ossmann. I didn't see you initially in the ER, but I'll be checking in on you for the next day or two. How's the shoulder? Less swelling?" He was in his late twenties, doing things by the numbers. He had dark wavy hair and thin dark glasses. He listened to Bodie's heart, despite the monitor, and pulled some X-rays out of a file on the door.

"How'd you break your ribs, anyway? At the mall?"

Bodie's parents slowly turned their heads toward Bodie, looking almost mad. "I broke them? Oh. I guess it was against Max Kolbe, over a week ago..."

The doctor looked annoyed. "You've been running around and playing football with broken ribs? You kidding me? They gotta hurt..."

"Only when I breathe."

Dr. Ossmann began to type onto a keyboard mounted to the far wall. "We'll get you something for the pain. There will be a grief counselor in tomorrow. But in the meantime I think you're going to need some more sleep, okay?"

"Look, Bodie, we're going to let you get some rest. We'll let you visit with Chrissy some. But they're going to even chase her out of here in 15 minutes. Get some rest, you'll see your friends tomorrow, okay?"

"Yeah dad. I'm... not going anywhere."

After they all had left, Chrissy rolled closer. "Truth is, they will probably let you go home in a day or two. Just do good on the grief counselor examination. I think that's what they're really worried about."

"Nobody has talked about my bicep and shoulder. I don't think that's a good thing."

Chrissy held his hand and kissed it. "This season is shot to hell. In the meantime, rest. Get better." She pet his shoulder as if it would act as therapy.

Although Bodie was with his parents, he knew he would see some additional visitors this morning, but was amazed to see Dean Horner.

"Hi, Bodie, how 'you doing?" Dean Horner was carrying a file. After some small talk, Dean Horner opened the file.

"I brought you your grades, Bodie. They were all turned in Friday, in person, or, in one case, Saturday, via Email." Dean Horner handed the carbonless sheet to Mrs. Houge.

"Bodie," started Mrs. Houge. Bodie braced for the worst. "You got a 3.0. If you averaged it out with that 1.8 from last year, you get... you get... what do you get?"

"A solid 2.4, Mrs. Houge. Good enough to keep participating in high school sports at Altamont High."

"And a good chance to build on it for college admission." Added Mr. Houge.

Bodie was dumbfounded. "Is there some kind of sympathy vote going on here? I can't believe I got the 'B' average."

"No," stated Dean Horner, now more serious than ever. "We don't do that. We don't fudge grades. Besides, they were all handed in before the shooting. None of the instructors had a chance to feel sorry for you. Mr. Parks e-mailed his in Saturday, but I doubt if he had any idea about a shooting at the mall, let alone that you might be in it. No. How could he have known?"

Bodie was sly. He acted dumb. He acted resigned.

"'C' in history, 'D' in Sociology." Mr. Houge scowled momentarily. "A- in English!" blurted Mrs. Houge, genuinely proud.

"'A-' in Art... and an 'A-' in... word processing?" Bodie thought Mr. Parks was buying his silence. Who cared? 'A-'... he would take it.

"Typing mom, that's all it is. Typing."

"Oh. Well, you did well, Bodie. I'm so proud of you." With that she kissed his head.

"We should be going. We keep going over the two limit. We'll check in on you tomorrow.

With that, Dean Horner said goodbye and left with the parents. 'Dang,' thought Bodie. 'I can play football now.' He felt the large rigid bandage mounted to his bicep with a drip line draining fluid out of it. He rubbed it thoughtfully, knowing his football career was over for now.

Around noon, Mr. Parks stopped by, with a bag from McDonalds.

"Hey Bodie. Guess I timed it right."

"Mr. Parks. Good to see you."

"'Get your grades?"

"Yup. You bumped me up a grade, didn't you Mr. Parks?"

"Bodie..., I know you're not the least bit interested in my private life, but, the truth is, Mrs. Horner and I have been seeing each other for about a year now. I was very single and she was..., well, married to Mr. Horner." They began to smirk and roll their eyes. Bodie would agree on this one.

"We didn't plan on anything. He left her all alone at a Parent's Night meeting and I just went over to say hello and keep her company. Mr. Horner went off with a group of boosters and the basketball coach. I felt awkward and sorry for her. I wasn't making any moves or anything. Turns out, we're both the same age... almost to the same month. Horner is about 13 years older than Janet. That's her name, Janet. Anyway, we hit it off, believe it or not. Turns out we both went to some Duran Duran concerts at the same time and didn't even know it. Corny, I know, but..." Mr. Parks paused for a moment, realizing he was justifying the break-up of a marriage. "She was miserable. It was that bad. They had no kids. She had had it. She was bailing out regardless what I was gong to do. I was in love at this point. I wasn't going anywhere. By this time, we were ready to be seen in public. Here. In Altamont. We had been going to Livermore and San Ramon to go out, but I think we wanted to be caught. To be seen. Until we saw you. Then we kinda freaked out. We were going to go to the Holy Grail Pizza Pub and have a Pizza and some beer. But after we saw you, we just headed for the door. I felt like a putz, we felt cheap and like we were sneaking around, all over again. We went to my place with our hands on our hips. We were 'there'. It had come to a head. Was she going to get a divorce? Were we going to be an 'Item'?" I babbled on that I wanted to get married and whatever she wanted to do. You know what? She did too!" Mr. Parks laughed. He was genuinely happy.

"I know you think this is really stupid, Bodie, but we decided that the little teeny weeny incident with you was the straw that broke the proverbial camel's back. We professed our love for each other, we decided to get a ring, she was going to ask for a divorce the very next morning. And then we turned on the T.V." Mr. Parks stopped. He stood up and shook his head, He held up his hands and was about to speak, but no words came out.

"Bodie; if you were not there, and we went to the Holy Grail Pizza Pub, we would have gone to the back nook area. They found something like eight dead bodies there. I swear to god; we were going to sit right there. We would have died there. There's no doubt about it. I told Janet right then and there you saved our lives. In a way, you saved our lives two different ways. Sometimes life gives you a great big slap in the face to live your life the way you see fit. It happened that night, that's for sure, for us. And when we sat there, dumbfounded, watching a body count going up and up and up. I remembered I hadn't sent in my grades yet for Business and for Word Processing. I wondered if you were even alive. I told Janet about you and your plight for being eligible for playing football, and she yelled out 'A! A-! But, A!'"

Mr. Parks stood up, seemingly exhausted. He shook Bodie's hand and said, "Thanks. Enjoy your hamburger."

"Just what the doctor ordered." Bodie chomped on the not-so-healthy Big Mac and fries. "Thanks for moving my 'B' up to an 'A-'."

"'B'? You were right on the line of 'D+' 'C-'," said Mr. Parks, as he walked out of the room, shaking his head.

Bodie savored the Big Mac as it blended it's magical secret sauce burgerness with the basic fries' potato starch into a gastrointestinal melange of epicurean ecstasy.

"Yup," chomped Bodie. "I can play football, all right."

Bodie woke up; only three hours had passed since Mr. Parks had left. He tried to prop himself up on the pillow behind him so he could watch some T.V. A man walked in and grabbed the control to the bed. It raised high enough to sit upright, but still rest on a soft, fluffy pillow.

"'Better?" he asked. He was a man in his mid twenty's. He had black hair, neatly combed back, executive style.

"Jake? Jake! It is you. You look... nice..." said Bodie, slightly bewildered.

"Yeah. I'm all cleaned up. No more undercover at the mall. My 'cover' has been blown, to say the least. But, hey, my assignment came in anyway. I'm going to the Pacific Rim. I am ready to go tropical. Plus I can use all my training now. Guns and everything. And the pay is, like, triple."

"I'm happy for you. I think you were born to do this. I'm glad they're sending you in."

"Yeah, well, I am happy and all, 'cept for all the people that didn't make it. I'm sorry about your friends. And I'm really sorry about your arm. No football?"

"No football. You were right about the full metal jacket. It didn't shred my tissue like a hollow tip would have. I guess I have that to be thankful for. Who knows? Maybe I could play some JUCO football next year."

"That's the spirit. Keep chasing that dream Bodie. I mean it."

They began to talk football and college, even the military. Bodie realized they were talking about life itself, and what you make out of it.

After a while, Jake stood up. "I've gotta go. I've got some passport business to attend to in Stockton. 'Gotta get my ducks in a row. But just to let you know, Bodie; the guy that shot you, the one with the ecology symbol? It was Commander Plastique. We got 'em, Bodie. And quite frankly, if you weren't spotting for me, well, I'd be dead. No doubt. Probably your friends with the rocks, too. You saved their lives, man. I'm not saying that to make you feel better. It's just the plain truth. It cost you your arm, for now, but your help kept the body count down by at least fifteen. No lie."

Bodie offered his left hand. They shook awkwardly. "Good luck in Brunei or wherever you're going..."

"You better believe it. The natives are real friendly, man..." Jake said with a sly laugh. With that, he was gone. A minute later C.J. And Jocko finally arrived, and within moments, Chrissy.

C.J. and Jocko brought a pizza with them. Surprisingly, Bodie was famished already.

"Food for the soul. Sweet sausage for the mind and all that," said Jocko. Bodie did not recognize the pizza box. It would be a while before he would be able to buy a Holy Grail Pizza in Altamont.

"Nobody told you guys the results of the commission!" ejaculated C.J., as if the thought hit him out of the blue, in mid-bite. "They got Coach Crutchfield fired. It was a big suspension, almost a year, and he just quit. Plus Charter Stockton had to forfeit every game except the first one of the season, before they got those LA guys."

"Whoa," blurted Bodie, with a mouth full of pizza in his mouth. "So we won. We won the Charter Stockton game?"

"Yup. We're going to CIF, unless Hester, like, really screws up. But she's taking snaps and running through plays. I think she can pull it off."

"The next two teams are cellar dwellers. We're in. I don't care what Ramsey says," pronounced Jocko in between bites.

Bodie wanted to warn him about over confidence, but he didn't. Nothing would stop this team, not now.

"You know, half the school's girls were wearing the medieval T-shirt you designed," said Jocko. "C.J. ran off, like, two hundred for any girl that brought in a white tee. It was a sign of support for Bodie Houge. The Chronicle came in and took pictures... put them on the front page."

"Above the fold!" added C.J..

As Bodie ate with his friends and Chrissy, he thought about what Mr. Parks had said and all the pain he and Mrs. Horner went through to finally be together. Here Bodie was with the girl he loved, and with friends he came so close to losing. He didn't know how he knew it, but he knew he would play football again, some day.

EPILOGUE
ON THE FIELD OF RIVER ISLAND

IT WAS AUTUMN, THE SUN CAST LONG SHADOWS
over over the gently rolling lawn at River Island Community
College. Bodie and Chrissy were lying on the grass, making
small talk. It was late in the afternoon, and the Delta Breeze
was kicking up. It felt good in Bodie's face. He had just
showered after practice, and was trying to cool off.

"Coach Boone told me not to be afraid to drill a pass
really, really hard; that these guys could take it. Can you
believe that? It's the complete opposite of what Coach
Ramsey was telling me all of the last season season at
Altamont. Sheesh."

"Good. It seems to have made your day..., you're really
smiling today." Chrissy said with a laugh, slightly squinting
at Bodie's expression.

"Well, Coach Boone also said that Saturday night's
game is going to have a couple of scouts from San Diego
State and San Jose State. And they're not looking for
linemen, if you know what I mean." Bodie tilted his head for

emphasis.

"Wow. Great. Maybe we can get out of the heat of this valley!"

"Yes, we can." Bodie repeated, shining the diamond on her ring with his thumb.

"Hey you guys, quit getting all mushy." It was C.J. walking up with Jocko. They finally finished their showers. "We have a big game tomorrow night."

Chrissy recoiled to her study position. Bodie's ever-present sheep dog had returned. But she didn't mind. He was the child they didn't have yet. He was part of the family.

"See the paper? Hester is on the front page, and above the fold!"

"Isn't she always on the front page?" retorted Bodie, almost bored of the superstar Hester.

"Not of the sports section, on the front page of the Chronicle! It's Homecoming and they're 7-0, man. Should we go tonight?"

It had been almost two years since the Mall shooting; Bodie did not go to any football games last year, his first year out of high school. But little by little he did better in his junior college grades and then last summer Coach Boone got him to try out for the quarterback position. He won it hands down, his arm was stronger than ever, thanks to therapy and weight training. Best thing of all, he was only now burning the first year of his college eligibility. If he transferred, he could play for three more years. As big as C.J. and Jocko were, they were the smaller men on Bodie's offensive line. He had tools on this team, all around.

"Tonight, huh?" said Bodie, looking at Chrissy out of

the side of his vision.

"Whoa!" exclaimed Jocko. "'You actually thinking of going back to a Highlander ball game?"

"Yeah. Maybe it's time."

"Homecoming. It's the time to do it," said Chrissy, with a broad smile erupting on her face. "You missed the Bonfire. People were all asking about you, man," said C.J.. "Hey look..., it's Melissa and you know who!"

C.J. ran over to a little toddler in bib overalls walking mechanically toward Bodie's gang. "There's our little big man!"

Melissa laughed and let little Chase run over to C.J. and Jocko. She and Chrissy were almost finished with their medical classes. Melissa was getting her radiology certificate and Chrissy was going to be an Registered Nurse within another year. After which they could go just about anywhere. For Chrissy that would be about a foot from wherever Bodie wound up.

Chrissy stared at Bodie as the rest of the gang played with Chase. "Earth to Bodie..., what on earth were you thinking about?"

"Oh, I was thinking about Chase. Big Chase, and..." his voice trailed off. He had thought of Chase, it was impossible to do otherwise with the little Chase around, but only for a second. His mind had wandered off into a long dead world where every person was an obtuse character in his own right, trying to live a life in the shadow of an edifice that shaped their lives almost as much as the Mall had shaped his.